Casa da Branca

Casa da Branca

Rosie Vidovix

St Ursin Press

First published in Great Britain in 2017
by St Ursin Press, 3 Broadfield Court,
1-3 Broadfield Road, Folkestone, Kent CT20 2JT,
United Kingdom

Cover picture by Jane Spencer
(janespencer.com)

ISBN 978-0-9955730-0-0

St Ursin Press is an imprint of Trencavel Press
www.trencavel.co.uk/St Ursin.html

Your story won't go untold

Branquinha

When Dona Branca, the owner of the brothel, nicknamed the new girl Branquinha everyone knew she was Dona Branca's protégée and that no one should mess with her.

That was unlikely to happen though because she was petite and her big brown eyes had nothing but innocence in them and her quiet and modest manners, a very uncommon quality among prostitutes, were welcomed by most people.

It was her first time as a 'proper girl'. In the past, her lovers had given her enough money to help her out, but she had never been to a house of ill repute before. When Branquinha decided to follow that way of life, she caught the coach and travelled as far as it would go and at the end of the road she found herself in Jardim do Ouro, a small gold-mining village in the middle of the Amazon rainforest, and a place most people had never heard of.

At the brothel, everyone knew what Branquinha was about to go through and they pitied her. She looked out of place among the other women, who were a lot more experienced. Time had etched its toll on their faces and their bodies had been abused by years of alcohol, late nights and all sorts of mistreatment by the men who came to 'make love' with them.

Murilo, the young gay bartender and manager, too, felt sorry for Branquinha, but he also realised her potential: she was naïve and young; had clear, light and delicate skin; long dark hair and straight white teeth. He knew she would be good for business.

Murilo, in his outrageously camp voice, explained to Branquinha how it all worked: the man paid for the 'key', which allowed him the use of Branquinha's room for thirty minutes. That money was paid in advance directly to the house. The client would pay extra if he stayed overnight.

'If the guy doesn't have enough time to finish what he came here for, tell him to come back again another time,' Murilo advised Branquinha. 'Any money he gives you is yours to keep, but you must always ask for the money in advance unless they are regular clients.'

'What if he doesn't...'

'Even if he doesn't!' Murilo interrupted. 'Also, ensure you keep your money safe and make sure you have all your important documents and any valuables in a box in case you need to leave in a hurry.'

'Why would we need to leave in a hurry?' Branquinha asked, worried.

'Sister, we're almost on top of the River Jamanxim! When it floods, we won't have much warning before we have to leave the building. Last year, I wasn't ready in time and lost the only picture I had of my mother.'

There was a lot to learn about drinks. If one of Branquinha's clients – she didn't have any yet but she should expect many, she was told – ordered a bottle, she would get five per cent commission. She would also get twenty per cent commission on cocktails but none on beer or cachaça, the strong rum-like drink.

'I make the cocktails, so yours will have no alcohol in it. Dona Branca doesn't like the girls drinking spirits,' Murilo warned Branquinha. 'Drunken girls are bad for business.'

'Every time you are done, you must have a shower.' Murilo showed Branquinha the two bathrooms. 'Dona Branca doesn't like dirty girls.'

'Where do we wash our clothes?'

'Branca likes the girls to have beautiful finger nails so she pays for a laundry lady to wash all our clothes.' Murilo held Branquinha's hand and examined her nails. 'Nails like yours won't do. Ask Carmem to teach you how to do a manicure. She is good at it and you will save money.'

As they passed the kitchen they couldn't get in because Zulmira, the cook, had not arrived yet and the kitchen was kept locked.

Through the crisscross partition they looked in.

'Zulmira must be a good cook.' The kitchen reminded Branquinha of her mother's kitchen where everything was very clean and neat and the aluminium pans were as shiny as a mirror.

'Zulmira is a very good cook,' Murilo replied. 'She makes the best fish casserole in the whole of Jardim do Ouro.' Murilo's voice was quite loud so Branquinha stood back. 'For your birthday she will make you a lasagne and bake you a cake,' Murilo continued until Branquinha was suitably impressed.

'Does Zulmira live here too?' Branquinha asked.

'She used to but she couldn't get proper sleep at night so she moved out.' Murilo looked at Branquinha as if the answer was obvious. 'Zulmira lives with her lover up the road.'

Branquinha made a mental note of every word Murilo told her. 'Lunch is at twelve and dinner at six. Eat your dinner fast because we open at six-thirty and although most clients will only arrive after eight, you can pick up extra business if you are there early.'

'If you want to send money to your family the best way is to pay it in at Zé do Ouro, the gold trader across the road and they will pay into the account you want.'

'What about the post office?'

'The post office?' Murilo laughed. 'There are very few post offices in the jungle, sister, and none in Jardim do Ouro.' Murilo closed his eyes as he spoke. 'The nearest post office is in Moraes de Almeida, the town you passed before getting here, forty kilometres away. The best way for you to get letters from people is by asking them to write to the head office of the gold trading shop and they will send the letters in the money bag.'

'Is it safe?'

'Safe?' Murilo laughed. 'Sister, all the money that comes into Jardim do Ouro comes from the gold trading shop because they bring in the money to buy gold and all the money ends back at their shop after all. They are also the only place we have around here where we can send money home.'

From the porch, Murilo pointed to the shop across the street. 'Zé do Ouro, the manager, is a nice guy. You can trust him...' Murilo stopped suddenly before adding, 'as much as you can trust anyone in this place.'

Branquinha was glad to know she had a safe way to send money to her mother.

'You can borrow these bed sheets until you have enough money to buy your own.' He gave her a few sheets and a faded red chenille bedspread. 'You'll also need this.' Murilo handed her a white enamel chamber pot.

Branquinha spent the rest of the afternoon cleaning her new windowless bedroom and making the bed with the sheets Murilo had lent her.

She removed all the spiders and moths from the walls, washed the floor and burnt some cardboard to get rid of the mosquitoes that buzzed in the room.

Branquinha brushed the smelly mattress with fabric conditioner and Zulmira gave her some oil to rub on the bed to keep the woodworm away from the wood.

When she'd finished the cleaning, she lit the incense that Dona Branca had given her. 'This incense is made of red roses and it's great to attract business.'

Branquinha prayed that Branca was right and she, soon, would get enough money to send to her mother.

The Customer

On Branquinha's first night, Dona Branca sent a message to a rich local merchant telling him there was a virgin girl in the house.

'He's the local engine dealer. Every time a machine breaks in this place, it's his shop that people go to,' the madam explained. 'He'll pay well for tonight.'

Just before he arrived, Dona Branca gave Branquinha a solution to put in between her legs.

'But I'm not a virgin,' Branquinha replied.

'Never mind, dear. This will make it tight,' the older woman explained.

When the merchant arrived, a fat and ugly man with a moustache that covered most of his mouth and face, Dona Branca took him to the Red Room – a room where the uneven wooden walls were covered by red satin fabric. The bed had red fresh linen. The large rug, although old, covered the gaps on the wooden floor stopping the smell and the cold coming from the mud and stagnant water beneath the building. The Red Room had an en-suite bathroom and Dona Branca took great pride in it, as it was the only brothel's room in the whole of the Jardim do Ouro that had such a luxury.

The merchant took his clothes off and Branquinha had to cover her mouth to hide her shock: he had a stomach that was bigger than the biggest watermelon she had ever seen. She hoped he wouldn't crush her under his weight. As he fumbled with her small breasts, wanting to kiss her mouth, she could smell the garlic, onion and everything else he'd had for dinner.

'I don't kiss on the mouth!' She remembered what Murilo had

said about not kissing on the lips.

The merchant was excited; after all, a virgin was not something he had everyday and three minutes later he was finished. He got up, put his trousers back on and handed Branquinha a wad of notes.

As the merchant walked away with a self-satisfied grin on his lips, Branquinha went to shower. She washed and washed and if it wasn't for someone knocking on the door hurrying her, she would have stayed there a long time, for no water would ever be enough to wash away the dirt she felt inside.

Jardim do Ouro

Branquinha's first overnight client left very early in the morning and she got up to open the front door for him.

She heard a cockerel in the distance but the few street dogs lying on the middle of the road were the only living creatures you could see outside.

The sun was beginning to appear behind the tall trees in the distance. Branquinha wondered how mankind found reasons to go to the most distant and unhospitable places digging their way in by force and obliging everyone and everything out of their way. *How many trees did they have to fell to make this road, to make this place?*

She stood on the open porch, a sort of veranda, fenced with a low banister on each side, and painted in turquoise blue, while the floor was simply made from rough wooden planks.

Across the road, Branquinha saw the building of the rival brothel, The Palace. Lodged between the pharmacy and the gold trading shop the brothel was slightly taller than the other buildings, but even with its bright yellow walls and a large gold sign above the door, the building was still less grand than Casa da Branca.

Up the road, there was the Restaurante da Dijé, the place where Murilo bought his snacks in the afternoon.

Branquinha looked further up and couldn't see the end of the road she'd travelled from. She knew that the narrow dusty road started twenty kilometres away in Moraes de Almeida – the nearest town with a post office, a bank and a large landing strip.

On her right, there was the River Jamanxim, over two hundred metres wide, dark and ready to swallow anything that dared to challenge its power.

Branquinha remembered Zulmira's advice the previous afternoon *'Keep away from the river because if you don't get killed by the caimans, piranhas and boa constrictors, the water will drown you.'*

Pequena

When Zulmira arrived to prepare breakfast, Branquinha was still sitting outside, upset from the previous night. She followed Zulmira to the kitchen and when the cook offered her a slice of soft homemade bread and butter, Branquinha chewed on it for a long time, her throat not yet ready to swallow it. She watched Zulmira, scrubbing a pan, singing along with the song on the radio. From time to time, Zulmira would swing her large bottom from side to side, dancing with the music.

When the commercial break came on, Zulmira asked Branquinha, 'Was it all right last night?'

Branquinha couldn't answer; instead, she nodded.

'Don't worry dear, it will get better.' Zulmira cleared Branquinha's empty cup and wiped the crumbs off the table. 'Why don't you help me with these beans?' And she poured two cups of dry beans on to the wooden table.

'I have here a letter from Maria who offers the next song to her mother...' Zulmira switched the radio off.

'Please don't turn it off on my account.'

'It's all right.' Zulmira split the pile of beans into half. 'That song makes me sad and I don't like sad songs.' She pushed half of the beans towards Branquinha. 'Life is sad enough as it is.'

Branquinha didn't reply.

'How did a pretty girl like you end up in a godforsaken place like this?' Zulmira started making a small pile of the unwanted beans, her black fingers working fast. 'How old are you?'

'I'm going to be twenty-three soon.' Branquinha didn't mind Zulmira's questions.

9

'You should be married to a nice man and not in a brothel, young lady.' Zulmira's tone didn't sound reprimanding to Branquinha but concerned.

'Well...'

'I know. You had no choice.' Zulmira answered her own question. 'My mum has heart palpitations.'

Zulmira stood up and poured a glass of water from the terracotta water tank in the corner and gave the glass to Branquinha.

'I have no father and between my mum and me, we couldn't make enough money to send her to see the specialist,' Branquinha replied.

'How come you are not married?'

'All the young men in my town knew I wasn't a virgin.' Branquinha confided in Zulmira.

'What about a nice older man?'

'Oh them...' Branquinha picked some rotten beans out of the pile before answering. 'There were some that were nice to me and sometimes they gave me money, but nobody wants to marry spoiled goods who is also bringing an old and sick lady to come and live with them.' Branquinha sipped the water.

Zulmira had heard the same story a hundred times.

'The town where I live, Glória de Dourados, is very small,' Branquinha added.

'How far is it from here?' Zulmira asked.

'I'm not sure. I know it's over two thousand kilometres,' Branquinha replied. 'With the roads being so bad, it took me almost ten days to get here.'

'Why did you come so far?' Zulmira asked.

'I didn't want anyone to know...' Branquinha picked some bad beans from her pile and pushed them to one side.

'How did you get here? This is where the devil lost his boots and didn't come back to collect them!' Zulmira laughed at her own joke.

'I got a coach up to a point, but then I ran out of money so I got a lift with a lorry driver. On the coach, I sat next to a miner who told me about Jardim do Ouro and Dona Branca.' Branquinha tucked her hair behind her ear. 'I'm so glad Dona Branca took me in.'

'Branca is a good woman and she looks after the girls like they were her own daughters,' Zulmira said.

Branquinha didn't point out that a mother would not have her daughters working in a house of ill repute. She knew what Zulmira meant.

Zulmira joined Branquinha's beans with her own. 'Make sure you take the pill every night so you don't get pregnant and you will be fine.' Zulmira got up. 'You're pretty and if you save wisely you'll soon be going home with enough to look after you and your mum.'

'Zulmira!' They heard someone shouting from the corridor.

'Shush, Pequena,' Zulmira hushed the young girl who came into the kitchen. 'You'll wake Cloé and Dona Branca.' Zulmira pulled a box down from a cupboard. 'Sit down. I'll make you a hot chocolate.'

The girl sat at the table, smiling, her large green eyes staring at Branquinha. 'You are the new girl!'

'Yes.' Branquinha smiled back.

'I'm Pequena,' the younger girl said biting on the slice of bread Zulmira had given her. 'They call me Pequena because I'm the youngest one and I'm short. I won't be here for much longer. Soon my boyfriend, Martinho, will be eighteen and he will come and marry me.'

'Nice to meet you.' Branquinha smiled at Pequena again.

'Branquinha is a good nickname for you. You are so white,' Pequena said putting her arm next to Branquinha's and comparing their skin colour.

'You have beautiful olive skin,' Branquinha replied. 'I'm too white.'

'Have you met Ana, Carmem and Cloé?'

'Don't talk with your mouth full, Pequena,' Zulmira interrupted. 'You know it's rude.'

'Sorry,' Pequena apologized, wiping her mouth on her sleeve.

'I met a few girls, but I can't remember their names,' Branquinha said. 'There were so many of them.'

'Carmem is from Paraguay and she's my favourite but I like Ana too. Ana helps Zulmira bake bread,' the young girl explained.

'Ah, I did meet them'

'How about Cloé? Have you met her?' Pequena lowered her voice. 'She is the slim one with short hair on the sides and all curly on the top, like a bird's nest. She is not nice.'

'Pequena, you'll get in trouble with Cloé. You know what she is like!' Zulmira said.

'Cloé's fast asleep. She doesn't wake up until lunchtime. Besides,' the young girl looked at Zulmira, 'you said Cloé never has anything nice to say about anyone.'

'Pequena! Eat your breakfast and stop talking.' Zulmira looked at Branquinha and said, 'Youngsters!'

Branquinha laughed.

Pequena finished eating her slice of bread. 'This is a nice hot chocolate. Branquinha, would you like to try some?'

'No thanks...'

Pequena finished drinking the hot chocolate and left the kitchen.

'Thank you!' Zulmira shouted from the kitchen.

'Thank you, Zulmira.' Pequena came back to thank the cook.

'You are welcome, Pequena.' When Zulmira replied the girl was already running down the corridor and too far to hear the older woman.

'Is she Dona Branca's daughter?'

'No, dear, she's not.' Zulmira pressed her lips tightly together. 'She is one of the girls.'

'But she's so young!'

'Fourteen.' Zulmira sighed.

'Fourteen? Don't the police care?'

'Sergeant Armando came once and even after Dona Branca told him about the scars on Pequena's back from her father's beatings he wouldn't let her stay,' Zulmira explained.

Branquinha looked at Zulmira, waiting for the rest of the story.

'He only changed his mind when Dona Branca's man, João Preto, took Pequena to the police station with him, actually showed him Pequena's scars and told Sergeant Armando that whipping and burning was not the only damage her father did to her.'

'The poor child is haunted by it,' Zulmira carried on. 'She often hurts herself and wants to die.'

Zulmira touched her forehead, heart, left and right shoulders blessing herself with the shape of the cross. 'Our Lady in Heaven, bless his other children!'

'So the police do know then?' Branquinha asked again,

incredulous that the police would allow someone so young to be a prostitute in a brothel.

'In the end Sergeant Armando agreed with João Preto that she'd be better off here than being sent to live with a monster like her father. We all hope that Martinho, this boy she is in love with, comes and rescues her out of this life.'

'Where is he now then?' Branquinha asked Zulmira.

'He works with his dad on one of João Preto's mines about thirty kilometres after you cross the river.' Zulmira poured the beans into the pressure cooker and then put the radio on again.

And at that moment, Branquinha understood it was better to be fatherless than to have a father like Pequena's.

The Shower

Branquinha woke up before her customer and her nostrils filled with the strong smell of sweat. She wasn't sure if it came from her or the client. She got up as quietly as she could and wrapping herself in a towel, she headed to the shower.

It was very early and Murilo had not got up to wash the bathrooms yet so Branquinha brushed the dirt on the floor from the previous night before she stepped in the shower with her rubber flip-flops on.

The water, which was pumped from the river the night before, was cold, but Branquinha welcomed it when it hit her skin. She came from a place where the summer was very hot, but Branquinha had not expected to encounter this heat in June.

'There are two seasons in the jungle,' Murilo had told her the day before, 'summer, when everything is dry and dusty and winter when it rains every day all day. If you don't make enough money during summer then forget it because work dies off to almost nothing in winter.'

Washing her hair, Branquinha reminded herself that nothing made sense in Jardim do Ouro and the weather was no different.

She got back to her room and the client was still asleep. She didn't know what to do so she sat in bed leaning against the headboard wishing she wasn't there. *I'm here because it is the only way to help my mum,* Branquinha reminded herself.

Branquinha heard a cockerel from somewhere in the village followed by another one. They reminded her of home and Branquinha thought about her mother. By this time of the morning she would be up feeding the chickens...

Branquinha's mother was a good woman, but life had been

unkind to her. Her mother's parents had died when she was still a child and she and a younger sister were brought up by a strict aunt. As soon as she could, her mother's sister got married and left home. Her mum stayed behind and looked after her aunt for years and just before the old lady died, her mum got married.

Branquinha's memory of her dad were very faded, but she remembered a few times when he beat her and often her mother as well. When he ran away with the wife of another man who lived down the road, it was just a relief. Branquinha and her mother struggled with the bit of money that came in from washing richer people's clothes and so they managed to keep hunger away.

When Branquinha's mother fell ill, people from the church helped a lot, but help stopped coming because someone said Branquinha had been sleeping with her boyfriend.

Why did I do that? Branquinha asked herself while folding her client's T-shirt and jeans. *I wish I had saved myself for a good man who would marry me and help me look after my mum.* Branquinha's thoughts were interrupted by the client moving.

'You showered yourself for me?' he asked Branquinha rolling over and pulling her towards him.

When the client finished Branquinha got up and offered him a clean towel with his folded clothes on top and her box of toiletries. 'Use the shower on the left. I cleaned it earlier.'

The client left the room and Branquinha quickly stripped the sheets off the mattress. When he came back, Branquinha was sitting down on the bed, the rest of his things neatly tidied next to his bag.

'You are a sweet girl. If I wasn't married I would take you away from this life,' he said while putting his shoes on.

'I'm not planning to stay here for long.' Branquinha had never felt so ashamed of herself.

'Make sure you leave this place as soon as you can,' he said, giving her some money.

'You paid last night...'

'Girl, here is something you need to learn as soon as possible: never say no to money,' the client interrupted Branquinha. 'If you want to get out of here, you need all the help you can get. Besides, you deserve it.'

When Branquinha got to the kitchen for breakfast, Carmem, the Paraguayan girl was there.

'Are you all right?' Carmem asked, her voice slightly accented.

'I am.' Branquinha smiled shyly, not wanting to tell a stranger that she felt sick for lying with men she didn't even like.

'It is not easy at first but if you close your eyes and pretend you are making love with Julio Iglesias it might be easier!' Carmem threw her long black hair to one side and laughed.

'I don't really fancy Julio Iglesias, but I know what you mean.' Branquinha giggled, thinking it was funny, but not a bad technique after all. 'I'll give it a go.' She laughed again.

The Loan

In the afternoon, Branquinha asked Murilo if he would go to the gold trading shop with her.

'What for?' Murilo asked. 'Surely you've not made enough money to send home yet?'

'The merchant was generous and I had two other clients last night,' Branquinha explained and when she told Murilo how much she had made, Murilo opened his eyes wider.

'That's a lot of money, but you should wait a bit longer until you have a big lump sum so you don't pay the fees the gold shop charges to send money,' Murilo told her.

'My mum really needs the money,' Branquinha replied quietly. 'When I left, she was feeling very tired and even the small chores exhausted her and now that I'm not there, I worry that the heavier work will kill her.'

'Wait until Monday. Saturdays are very good for business,' Murilo suggested.

'I left two weeks ago. I can't afford waiting any longer.' Branquinha sat down on a chair and lowered her head, her eyes flooding with tears.

'I know what.' Zulmira, who was sitting in a corner, got up and walked towards Branquinha. 'You can borrow this from me so your mum will have enough to go to the doctor's and have some left.' Zulmira put her hand on her wide bosom and pulled a wad of notes from inside her bra and placed it in Branquinha's hand.

Branquinha didn't know what to say. She didn't want to accept Zulmira's generosity, but she knew her mother needed the money.

'Are you sure?' Branquinha asked Zulmira.

'Of course I'm sure.' Zulmira walked back to her chair and continued with her crochet work. 'That is what friends are for, isn't it?' she replied, looking from above her glasses resting on her nose. 'Thank you, Zulmira.' Branquinha hugged Zulmira. 'I'll pay you back as soon as I earn some more!'

Zulmira didn't reply but she knew Branquinha was not only thanking her for the money but also for the trust and friendship. Zulmira smiled.

You Are Who You Are

Branquinha had been in the village for almost a week, but hadn't been out of the Casa da Branca since her visit to the gold shop when she went to send the money to her mother.

Life in Jardim do Ouro was somehow different to everywhere else. Branquinha could not fathom how some people who came and stayed only an hour would be remembered for months, yet others, who had lived there for years, would be forgotten the day they left.

Branquinha could not help but notice that more people crossed the river from this side. She wondered where did they go, that so few came back.

Branquinha was still lost in thoughts when Zulmira and Pequena joined her on the porch.

'Let's go to the other side of the river,' Pequena asked Branquinha. 'I want to introduce you to my friend Dora. She lives in the big house and makes delicious fudges, of all sorts.' Pequena pointed towards the other side of the river. 'There is also the ice cream shop where Carmem works some days.'

From the porch, Branquinha had seen the two store buildings, unpainted, with large windows.

'Not today,' Branquinha replied, not ready to face the outside world just yet.

'Zulmira, tell Branquinha how good Dora's fudges are,' Pequena asked the cook.

'Why don't you want to go?' Zulmira put her arm around Branquinha's shoulder.

'I'm embarrassed. I'm a woman of easy virtue.' Branquinha looked down on the floor.

'My girl,' Zulmira said, 'don't be ashamed of who you are and what you are doing. What you need to realise is that life in a gold mining area is very different from anything you have seen before. In this place, nobody stands in judgement over others because this is a forgotten land where only people with nothing to lose run away to.'

Murilo

That morning the hot weather brought even more flies and ants to the kitchen and Zulmira was cursing the insects and also herself for not placing the bag of sugar into a proper container, when Pequena came running into the kitchen.

'Murilo's crying again!' Pequena announced as she sat at the kitchen table and grabbed the hot chocolate Zulmira placed on the table for her breakfast.

'Really?' Branquinha spread margarine on a slice of warm bread and passed it to Pequena. 'I've never seen a grown man crying.'

'You have only been here for a week, Branquinha. You don't know this, but Murilo is not a proper man.' Pequena picked an ant out of her bread before biting into it.

'What do you mean,' Branquinha looked at Pequena, 'he's not a proper man? He's small and looks young but he's twenty-four, older than me.'

'I don't mean it like that, Branquinha.' Pequena wiped her mouth with the back of her hand. 'I meant he cries because he's a girl trapped in a man's body.'

Branquinha looked at the younger girl. 'What do you mean?'

'Zulmira told me that some men have a girl inside their bodies and that is why they like boys.' Pequena didn't sound sure of herself. 'Isn't that true, Zulmira?'

'Put your glass in the sink and go, Pequena. I'll explain everything to Branquinha.'

'Help me select the beans,' Zulmira said after Pequena left the room. She carefully poured the dried beans into a pile on the wooden table.

21

'A girl trapped inside his body? That is a bit far-fetched, is it not?' Branquinha looked at Zulmira searching for answers.

'I explained it in that simple way so Pequena would understand and accept it better.' Zulmira paused. 'Murilo is a good boy, but he is gay and he has suffered his whole life for that.'

'Gay?' Branquinha frowned, knitting her eyebrows together.

'Yes, gay. He likes guys, not girls.'

'Really?' Branquinha asked. 'I heard about gay people, but I wasn't sure they really existed.'

'They are very real. And they suffer their whole life for being the way they are because people don't understand them.'

Zulmira and Branquinha continued to pick out the bad beans from the pile in silence and Branquinha could feel her brain working hard to make sense of it all.

'So they aren't just crazy people who lost their way in life?'

'No,' said Zulmira, 'they're like everyone else, except that they prefer sex with people of their own gender.'

Branquinha didn't reply.

Zulmira went on, 'Murilo suffered terrible rejection from his family for being gay and I know he is a little funny, but if you look in his past you'll understand him a lot better.'

Branquinha moved uncomfortably on her chair.

'Murilo comes from a very wealthy family,' Zulmira continued, 'and they lived in a small town in the state of São Paulo where his father is a well-known political figure and head of the ruling party. As the oldest son, Murilo was educated in the best schools money could buy and from a young age he was coached to take on his father's business.'

'And why is he here then?'

'Even though he went to the best schools and travelled round the world he was never a very masculine man. His dad tried hard to get him to like women, guns and cars, but all he wanted was to read, write poetry and talk to boys.'

'Ah, that explains why he's so well spoken.'

'When he was seventeen he was caught in bed with the maid's son doing hanky-panky. The maid was immediately dismissed and a few days later her son was found dead in a dam not far from where they lived.'

'Oh, my god!' Branquinha's eyes opened wide. 'Did he drown or...?'

'Drowning is what everyone said, but Murilo was not convinced. He thought his dad was responsible, so he packed his things and ran away to the maid's house.'

'Why the maid's house?'

'Murilo's mum died when he was young and the maid was like a mother to him. Unfortunately, when he got there, her husband told him he had only brought disgrace to their family and he had to go away.'

'Poor Murilo. But why does he like boys and not girls?'

'Branquinha,' said Zulmira, 'some people are born that way and nothing can change it. Murilo looks tough, but he has a heart of gold. He is what he is and we have to accept it.'

'I have never met a man who likes other men.'

'He's not the only one in the world who's like that, Branquinha. There are many people like this and they hide because otherwise they get punished by people around them, sometimes even killed.'

'That is so sad.' Branquinha sighed. 'What a life to have.'

'The story doesn't end there, Branquinha.' Zulmira paused while she poured the chosen beans into the pan.

'Murilo ended up in the red light district of a town not far from where they used to live,' she went on, 'and after a few months, his uncle turned up for a party and saw him. The uncle and his gang raped Murilo and beat him so badly he almost died.'

'The madam took him to his father's house,' Zulmira carried on, 'but when they got there, his father refused to have him in and Murilo ended up at the maid's house. For weeks the maid looked after him in a small back room without the husband noticing.'

Branquinha stared at Zulmira, her eyes wide open.

'When Murilo recovered,' Zulmira went on, 'he sold his expensive watch, disappeared from town and never went back.'

'But the other day he told us he sent money to his mum.'

'He sends money to the maid, Branquinha. She's the only mother he ever had.'

Branquinha looked at the table, feeling terribly sorry for Murilo.

Zulmira continued, 'Even in this land full of weird people Murilo is rejected. His sexuality is uncomfortable to most men and only a very few men accept him as a normal human being.'

'Zulmira, how come you are so understanding of his problems?'

'Ah, Branquinha, I'm a black woman and in my forty-seven years I have seen many people suffer discriminations of all kinds.'

'Why are people so unkind to others? What is it to them if they are black, white or prefer to sleep with men or women?'

'I guess some people find it difficult to deal with people who are different to them.' Zulmira spoke in the same gentle way Branquinha's mother spoke. 'Not everyone is mean and unkind, but those who are bring tremendous suffering to those who are different.'

Zulmira gathered the rest of the beans, stood up, filled the pan with water, placed the lid on the pressure cooker and locked the lid on. The beans were ready to cook.

Cloé

The heat on the following day was unbearable and the breeze that usually came from the River Jamanxim had disappeared, giving way to a wave of hot air. Even the street dogs had vanished to the cooler shaded spots under the houses.

Branquinha and Pequena were sitting on the front porch when they saw a black police car coming down the road.

'The fat one is Sergeant Armando,' Pequena told Branquinha when the dusty pick-up truck drove closer. 'Hope they don't come in today. Murilo doesn't like him coming in because he is allowed free drinks and all free drinks come out of Murilo's commission.'

'Let's go inside,' Branquinha said to Pequena, getting up and heading indoors.

As they moved inside, Branquinha saw the police car through the bead curtains. 'They are coming in,' she said to Pequena. 'Go and get Murilo.'

As Pequena hurried to the back of the house, Branquinha saw Sergeant Armando struggling out of the car, the large door too small for his even larger belly.

'Good morning, new girl,' Sergeant Armando said entering the room smoothing his moustache. 'Is Cloé available?'

'I'll go and check, sir.' Branquinha got up from her chair and started moving towards the corridor to fetch Cloé and was just about to knock on her door when she remembered Cloé was with a client.

Branquinha went back to the salon to find Murilo pouring some whisky into a glass. 'If Sergeant Armando keeps coming here, he will bankrupt me!'

'He asked for Cloé, but she has a client with her. What do I tell him?' Branquinha asked Murilo.

'He'll wait hours for Cloé, if he needs to,' Murilo said, heading towards the table where Sergeant Armando was sitting. Another policeman had joined him.

'This is Cabo Ivan, the newest member of the team and one day my successor,' Sergeant Armando said, tapping the younger man on the shoulder. 'Bring another whisky, Murilo.'

Murilo went back behind the bar and poured another dose of whisky. 'This is all I need, another bloody policeman using us as his local bar!' Branquinha heard Murilo muttering under his breath.

'Go and get Cloé,' Murilo told Branquinha, 'and I don't care who she is with!'

Much later, when Sergeant Armando had finished with Cloé and left dragging a drunk Cabo Ivan out with him, Branquinha asked Murilo 'Why is Cloé so popular? She is not that beautiful.'

'Because Cloé does everything,' the brothel manager replied.

'What do you mean "everything"?' Branquinha asked.

'Everything!' Murilo bent his head slightly to the left and opened his eyes wide, laughing.

'Like what?' Branquinha insisted.

'Sister, if you think all there is to sex is to lie down, open your legs and pretend you are enjoying it, think again!' Murilo laughed again, walking off without answering Branquinha's question.

Branquinha looked at Carmem who was sitting on a chair nearby, her foot on the table while she painted her toenails. 'What does he mean?'

'Some women will do a lot more than just laying-down sex,' Carmem explained while she examined her handiwork.

'What else there is to do?'

'Uhm...' Carmem giggled. 'Branquinha, a woman's body has three holes and some of them use them all.'

Branquinha looked at Carmem with her mouth open in disbelief. 'No!'

'I don't do any of that disgusting stuff, but Cloé does all that and more.' Carmem carried on, 'Some men like it rough, but that is

Ana's department.'

Branquinha didn't ask anything else as she was afraid of the answers.

Carmem didn't stop though. 'Didn't you see the bruises on Ana's wrist the other day? She got paid well for it.' The Paraguayan woman laughed.

Branquinha didn't reply. She was still shocked by Carmem's comments on Ana's wrist marks.

'Don't worry, *guapa*,' Carmem said. 'We're protected here.' 'Branca is very good to her girls and nobody will dare to hurt us in fear of João Preto, her man.'

'I have not met him yet,' Branquinha told Carmem. 'Does he come here often?' She was curious about the man who was, indirectly, responsible for her safety.

'Yes.' Carmem finished painting her toenails and stood up, her feet next to each other so she could compare the toenails. 'The empty room next to yours is actually his. Often his men come and sleep there if they are not sleeping with one of us or other women in the village.'

'How can he protect Branca if he doesn't live here and is away most of the time?' Branquinha wanted to know more.

'By fear ,of course.' Carmem didn't seem to mind all the questions. 'He is a very fair man but you really don't want to upset him. The stories you hear...'

'Like what?'

'Oh... you'll hear them in due course, Branquinha.' Carmem looked at Branquinha, her eyes almost threatening her. 'Meanwhile, don't ask questions about João Preto.'

'Aren't you afraid of him, of this place?' Branquinha dared to ask wondering how a girl as beautiful and exotic as Carmem had ended up in that place.

'Not really... I have seen worse.' Carmem was working on her manicure now, removing her cuticles. 'I left Paraguay when I was very young and a guy turned up with the promise of a singing contract in Rio.' Carmem stopped for a second and looked at Branquinha, 'Europe was supposed to be next but after a short singing tour with his "troupe", I almost died in a brothel in São Paulo.'

'What happened?'

'He left us in a brothel saying we would only stay there for a few days and for us to be nice to the owner. It turned out that he had sold us.'

Branquinha's mouth was open for ages before she asked the question. 'Sold you? Like a slave?'

'Yes, like cattle.' Carmem's reply was calm; as if she didn't care. 'We were forced to do all sorts of things and I thank God every day for leaving that hell.'

Branquinha wondered how someone could survive such an experience and still be as cheerful as Carmem. 'How did you manage to get out?'

Carmem opened the small bottle of red nail varnish and started painting her nails. 'The owner of the place made the mistake of buying the daughter of a rich man and the father tracked his daughter down to the brothel. The police came, arrested the guy, closed the place down and I was let free.'

'Why didn't you go back to Paraguay, back to your family?'

'First I wanted to but there was no money and I stayed in São Paulo for a while. It was hard to make money if you didn't have a pimp and when Dona Branca came along and told me about this place I decided to move here.' Carmem lifted her right hand looking for mistakes on her manicure. 'Here I can do the thing I love most: to sing.'

'I have now saved almost enough to buy a place in Paraguay.' Carmem went on. 'I want to turn it into a house of shows. Another few months here and I will have the money.' Carmem started painting the nails of her left hand. 'Hopefully, I'll stop other girls making the same mistake I made.'

Branquinha didn't say anything for a minute or so, as she reflected on her own inexperience and luck. 'You had a tough life, Carmem,' Branquinha finally said to the other woman.

Carmem had finished painting her nails. '*Guapa*, people can only hurt you if you let them. I'm lucky to have come out of it alive and now I'm here to tell the tale.' She closed the bottle of nail varnish. That night when Carmem did her Paraguayan Show – a mixture of singing and tango dancing – Branquinha's admiration was not for her beautiful soprano voice or the perfect steps on the dance floor, but for Carmem's resilience and ability to overcome the worst in mankind.

Gigi

It was another hot evening and they were all running late. The laundry lady had not delivered the clothes on time and they had no water in the tap because someone had left the hose running in the street when they were watering down the dusty road, so the water tank was empty.

'I had to go to the river to get a bucket of water to wash. Have you seen how dirty that water is?' Pequena was annoyed. 'I hope I don't get an itch from it.'

'Don't be stupid, Pequena,' Murilo replied, 'that's the same water that comes to your shower every day.'

'Not really. The shower head filters it and keeps all the dirt out of my skin.' Pequena tried to argue with Murilo.

Murilo rolled his eyes upwards. 'Some people make a point of being stupid.'

'I'm going to be late for my show!' Carmem complained, her accent slightly stronger. 'Do you know how long it takes to dry this much hair?' Carmem had undone her plait and was towel drying her dark and thick hair which reached her waist.

'Carmem, if you are going to dry your hair, get out of my kitchen. I have added enough seasoning to the food today!' Zulmira said. 'And you, Murilo, stop calling people stupid. It is so unkind!'

Branquinha and Carmem were the first in the salon. Murilo was filling the large freezer with beer.

When a small girl with short dark hair entered the room and sat down in a corner across the room, Branquinha glanced at Carmem.

'Gigi,' Carmem whispered covering her mouth.

'Is she new?' Branquinha whispered back.

'She's been away with her xodó[1], Davi.'

'Xodó?' Branquinha stared at Carmem.

'The man she loves and a kind of boyfriend.' Carmem looked discreetly at Gigi. 'She is a bit mad; she spends most of her days up the road looking after her kitchen garden.'

'She has a kitchen garden? What for?'

'Because I like Nature!' Gigi shouted from the other side of the room, still filing her nails. 'If you are going to talk about me, do so loud enough so I can hear it properly.'

'Gigi, you haven't met Branquinha yet, have you?' Murilo ignored Gigi's irritation and, grabbing Branquinha's arm, he dragged her towards Gigi. 'She arrived the day before yesterday.'

'How old are you?' Gigi asked Branquinha. 'This is my table. You can only sit here if I invite you,' Gigi added, not waiting for Branquinha to answer the question.

Murilo sat down on the chair across the table from Gigi and pulled Branquinha's shoulder, forcing her to sit down on a seat between him and Gigi. 'So how was the honeymoon?' Murilo asked Gigi.

'Oh, Murilo!' Gigi closed her eyes, immediately changing her tone. 'It was wonderful!'

'Was it?' Murilo crossed his legs and crossed his hands over his knees, his head bent slightly to the left.

'Yes! Davi treated me like a princess.' Gigi pressed her right hand on her chest, against her heart.

'Yeah, right!' Cloé came from nowhere. 'Next thing you'll tell us he will leave his wife for a whore.' Cloé took a long drag of her cigarette

'As a matter of fact, he is going to do that.' Gigi straightened her back and crossed her arms. 'He went home to tell her.'

'If that is true, why did he send you back here then?'

'Mind your own business, you poison snake!' Gigi shouted at the other woman.

Cloé blew the smoke out, her lips pouting a little longer than needed. 'You are so stupid!'

---

1 Pronounced shodoh.

Branquinha stared at Gigi's face and watched the tears flooding her eyes.

'You never know.' Murilo frowned at Cloé. 'These things can happen.'

'He took her to Cuiabá, by aeroplane.' Pequena joined in. 'And bought her a new dress and shoes.'

'He's rich, for God's sake.' Cloé laughed. 'What does a rich gold trader wants with a whore like you?'

'He is leaving his wife tonight!' Gigi shouted. A tear came down on her face and dropped on the front of her blouse just above her small breasts.

'If that's the case, why are you back here?' Cloé wouldn't let it go.

'Ignore her.' Pequena put an arm around Gigi's shoulders. 'He loves you. Don't you think so, Branquinha?'

'Uhm, I guess…' Branquinha hesitated.

'I know he loves me. I know he loves me,' Gigi repeated.

'Of course he does, Gigi.' Murilo stood up. 'And don't let anyone tell you otherwise.'

For the entire night the girls talked about nothing else but Gigi and Davi. Would he come or not?

As the girls started turning in for the night, and Murilo began to clear up, Gigi paced up and down the salon, waiting for Davi.

'You can't avoid customers every night, Gigi.' Murilo opened the window and threw the bag of rubbish into the river. 'Dona Branca will not be happy.'

'Murilo, can I have a beer for my room?' Cloé shouted from the corridor. 'Oh, dear, he didn't come after all, what a surprise!' she said to Gigi laughing.

Gigi didn't reply. Instead she smiled staring at the door where Davi, the gold trader, was standing, with a suitcase in his hand.

João Preto

The following afternoon Branquinha met João Preto. She was alone, sitting on the porch when he arrived, her legs tangled on the bead curtains which Murilo had thrown on the chair blocking the salon door while he cleaned it.

The tall man with very dark skin climbed off a blue pick-up truck and then up the steps to the port in one go and stopped in front of her, looking down at her legs, his expression demanding she moved them so he could get past.

'I'm sorry.' Branquinha apologised, pulling the strings out of the chair and sitting properly, her back very straight.

He looked into Branquinha's eyes and she felt like the man had put a spell on her, his big black eyes speaking to each cell of her brain telling her to never upset him.

Still not knowing who the man was but aware that he was not someone to cross, Branquinha asked him, 'Uhm... Are you looking for someone?'

The man didn't reply. He moved the chair out of the way, towards the corner opposite Branquinha and walked into the salon.

Later, when she found out who he was, Branquinha understood why people were so afraid of João Preto.

The Stampede

That day, the sun was harsher than usual and every plant longed for a drop of water. Occasionally, a gust of wind would swirl down the road and blow the dust around, sending a thick cloud of powder into the air, then to cover every surface in town.

Seu[1] Fernando, the man who sold cigarettes, soft drinks and cachaça in the kiosk across from the brothel, was hanging a red awning on the front of his place to make some shade so his customers would not roast alive.

Branquinha had just finished watering the street in a weak attempt to stop the dust getting inside the house.

'If everyone did the same outside their place we would have a lot less dust around,' Murilo said while he rolled the hose and hung it on the outside wall of the house.

A man riding a horse came down the road and headed to Seu Fernando's place.

'Look, Branquinha, a cowboy!' Pequena pointed towards the man with wide shoulders wearing a cowboy hat on the other side of the road. 'Let's go to Seu Fernando to buy a peanut bar.'

'Pequena, I told you to stop pointing at people,' Murilo said, pushing Pequena's arm down. 'Besides, why would Branquinha want anything to do with a cowboy? They've no money! We don't want them here. They will have to go to The Palace.'

'He's good-looking and Branquinha likes tall strong men. She could fall in love with him and he'd take her away from this life.'

'She won't be in "this life" much longer,' Murilo replied. 'And by the way, the cowboy isn't tall, we're short!' He and Pequena had

---

1 An abbreviation for Senhor (Mr)

been arguing about everything the whole day.

'Look, he's coming this way!' Pequena said loudly.

'Shush...' Murilo and Branquinha said at the same time.

The cowboy crossed the road towards the Casa da Branca. 'Good afternoon!' he said, taking off his hat. He smoothed his dark hair and climbed the steps to the porch.

'Hello there!' Murilo couldn't hide his attraction to the good-looking man.

'Tomorrow morning we're crossing the river with a herd of four hundred cows and I just wanted to make sure if you need to use the ferry in the morning. Please cross tonight and leave the car on the other side, or go on the first ferry in the morning because the ferry will be busy with us the rest of the morning.'

'What's wrong with having cars and cows crossing together?' Pequena asked.

'The herd can get disturbed by cars so it's better if the ferry carries only cows,' Branquinha answered, before the cowboy could open his mouth.

'Ah...' Pequena understood. 'And where are your cows?' she asked the cowboy.

'They're coming this way. They've just passed Aguas Claras Spring. They will be here early this evening.'

'But Aguas Claras Spring is just over one kilometre away!' Murilo exclaimed.

'The cows can't go too fast or they lose weight and so money.' Again, Branquinha answered before the cowboy had a chance.

'Branquinha, you are so clever.' Pequena smiled at the cowboy. 'She'd make a good cowboy's wife, this one!' Pequena tapped on Branquinha's shoulder. 'And she has no children.'

'Pequena,' Branquinha said, 'go inside and tell the others that we're having a cattle drive going through the village tomorrow first thing!' Branquinha sent Pequena inside before the younger girl could say any more.

'Would you like a beer?' Murilo offered. 'It's on the house.' He went into the salon hoping the cowboy would sit with them a bit longer.

'What's that noise?' Branquinha looked up the road.

'Jesus Christ, it's a stampede!' The cowboy jumped the banisters of the porch and started shouting at the top of his voice, '*Stampede!*' He crossed the road, untied his horse and galloped up the road. '*Get out of the road. A stampede is coming this way!*'

People started started shouting to each other and within a few seconds they were moving their bikes, chairs, closing doors and windows and in less than two minutes you could see the cloud of dust at the top of the road.

Seu Fernando lowered the window of his kiosk and started to undo the awning he had just put up.

Branquinha saw Dijé, the restaurant owner, struggling to push a motorbike into her restaurant and shutting the doors. Branquinha's eyes moved up the road and her heart stopped.

Murilo pulled the chairs inside the house and shut one leaf of the door. 'Come inside, Branquinha!'

'Oh my god, the deaf boy's in the street,' Branquinha shouted. 'Someone grab him!'

'Stampede! Get inside!' The cowboy got down from his horse and ran into the porch..

'He's deaf!' Branquinha screamed.

The lanky boy, about six or seven years old, stood in the middle of the road, trying to make sense of what the cowboy was trying to say but oblivious to the horrific noise of the cows charging towards him.

'Get out of the road now!' the man shouted at the child.

'The boy is deaf!' Branquinha yelled from inside.

This time the cowboy heard her.

'Oh my god, the cows will get him!' Branquinha cried.

The cowboy moved back to the steps of the porch. Taking his rope from his waist, swirled it in the air, and within seconds, the boy was being dragged to the porch while the cows ran past where he had stood, heading towards the water.

Branquinha, with her arms around the deaf boy who still had the rope tied around his body, stood close to the wall in the porch while Murilo and the cowboy watched the cows running towards their death in the deep waters of the River Jamanxim.

The Mother

'Look what you've done to my son,' the woman shouted at the cowboy. 'You could have killed him, you stupid moron.'

'Lady, your son was about to be killed!' the cowboy said.

'I'm going to report you to the police!' the woman shouted, pointing her finger at the cowboy.

'What are you going to report him for, Dona Cida?' Sergeant Armando appeared from nowhere, his size dominating the room. 'Maybe you'd like to report him for saving your son's life?'

'Look what he did to the boy...' Dona Cida pointed to the bruises and rope burns on the boy's arm. 'And that whore was trying to do things to my son. When I got here she was giving him sweets!' She pointed at Branquinha.

'This *lady* saved your son's life!' Putting his hands on Branquinha's shoulders, the cowboy replied before Sergeant Armando had time to. 'And she gave him sweets to calm him down because he would not stop crying for you.'

'She...' Dona Cida began.

'If it wasn't for the young woman and the drover here, your son would be dead by now,' Sergeant Armando said to Dona Cida. 'By the way, where have you been the past three hours?'

'He is a naughty... I was...'

'If you looked after your boy a little better, he'd never have been down here at all,' Sergeant Armando continued.

'He often disappears for hours.'

'There was a stampede and you didn't even bother knowing where your son was for the past few hours.'

'I...'

'I don't want to hear a thing,' Sergeant Armando interrupted her. 'You go to Father Domingos and get him to pray for everyone who helped save your son's life in Mass on Sunday.'

Dona Cida didn't try to argue this time.

'I will be there and I want to hear Father Domingos mentioning Dona Branquinha and you are…?' Sergeant Armando turned to the cowboy.

'Vilson Reis, at your service, sir.' The cowboy offered his hand and touched his hat with the other, respectfully.

Sergeant Armando nodded, then glanced at Dona Cida. 'You take your boy with you now, Dona Cida, and I'll see you at the Mass on Sunday,' said Sergeant Armando, He turned to Vilson. 'Today you lost a lot of cattle, but you saved a boy's life. We will drink to that.'

'Murilo, the best whisky in the house!' Sergeant Armando shouted, adjusting his trousers before he sat down at his favourite table.

Branquinha noticed Murilo rolling his eyes while pouring half a glass of whisky for Sergeant Armando. *Poor Murilo. All the drink Sergeant Armando has will come straight out of his commission!*

'Excuse me,' Vilson called over to Murilo. 'I'll have a beer instead.' 'If you don't mind, sir,' he said to Sergeant Armando, 'whisky gives me headache, so a beer will be fine.'

'A drover who can't take his whisky?' Sergeant Armando replied, swallowing his drink in one go. 'And what about you, young lady? Would you like to join me and have some whisky?'

'Dona Branca doesn't like the girls drinking whisky,' Murilo answered on Branquinha's behalf. 'Here, have some beer instead.' Murilo deposited a beer and two glasses in front of Vilson.

Sergeant Armando's whisky barely touched the sides of the glass before he ordered another one.

When the policeman ordered the third drink, Zulmira took pity on Murilo and came to his rescue. 'Sergeant Armando, we've a lot of beef. Would you like to have dinner with us tonight?'

'Oh, it is a bit early for me, thank you, Zulmira. I stopped at Dijé's earlier and she fed me with one of her delicious pizzas. I'm still full.' Sergeant Armando laughed tapping his stomach.

'It's not too early for me, though.' Vilson stood up. 'It was a hard day and my men have set up camp now and I'll be joining them.'

'A pleasure to meet you, Drover Vilson,' said Sergeant Armando wobbling on his feet. 'Next... next time you pass by, stop at the office and have a beer with me. But before you go, leave some beef for my boys at the police station, will you?'

'I'll see to it, sir.' Vilson shook Sergeant Armando's hand. Then, turning to Branquinha and nodding his head gently, he said, 'Lucinda.'

'Who's Lucinda?' Pequena whispered to Murilo.

'It's Branquinha's real name,' Murilo answered

'Oh, I never knew that. How does he know your real name?' Pequena narrowed her eyes and looked at Branquinha.

'I told him earlier when he asked me how I ended up living here.'

'I think you like the cowboy, don't you?' Pequena sounded excited.

'Didn't you hear Sergeant Armando? He is not a cowboy, he is a drover!' Murilo wiped the counter with a damp white cloth. 'And you are right, she likes him and what is more, he likes her. I wouldn't be surprised if he came back later.'

It was a quiet night and there were no clients for Branquinha that evening.

'What a day! I'm glad it's over,' Murilo complained. 'First the stampede, then Sergeant Armando comes and drinks all the whisky which means I have no commission this week and now an empty house.'

By eleven there was nobody left and Murilo and Branquinha started putting the chairs on the table.

'Young lady, you should go to bed now. Don't forget Dona Branca is taking you to the dentist in Moraes de Almeida tomorrow, first thing in the morning,' Branquinha reminded Pequena.

Branquinha had her back to the door and didn't see the drover coming into the salon.

'Ahem!' Murilo cleared his throat while staring at the door.

'I knew you were coming back, cowb...drover,' Pequena said just before she jumped off the table she was sitting on. 'You came to see "Lucinda". You like her, don't you?'

'Pequena!' Murilo and Branquinha said at the same time.

'OK, OK, I'm going to bed.' Pequena walked towards the corridor. 'Bran..., I mean "Lucinda", likes you too,' Pequena said before running away up the corridor with Murilo hot in pursuit.

'She's funny, that young one.' Vilson picked up a chair and put on the table. 'But she's right. I do like you.'

Branquinha blushed. 'We had a weird experience today and things like that make you think you feel things you don't usually feel.'

Vilson didn't reply. Instead, he carried on helping Branquinha putting the chairs upside down on the table with Branquinha feeling uncomfortable with the silence.

'I think we're done here.' Branquinha could feel Vilson's breath on her neck. She turned around and lowered her face, avoiding his eyes. 'Would you want to stay tonight?' she asked shyly.

'I would love to stay tonight.' Vilson placed his hands on her waist and brought her closer to him.

'It's thirty reals for the key,' she replied quietly, staring at his lips. 'I won't charge you anything, but I don't kiss.'

Vilson touched her chin with his fingers pulling her slim body closer to his. Their lips were very close and she could smell soap on his skin.

'Oh, that's too bad, Lucinda. Because there is nothing I want to do more than kiss you.'

The Sunset

While the more experienced drovers slowly ferried the surviving cows to the other side of the river, Vilson and the rest of his men finished taking care of the dead animals. The local butcher had come the previous day and helped clear the insides of the lifeless beasts but there was still a lot to do.

In the morning, Branquinha, Carmem, Ana and Zulmira helped out salting pieces of beef and hanging them in the sun so the water would come out and the flesh would become jerked beef.

Many miners, hearing about the disaster, came for some cheap and fresh meat. Any unsold meat would be packed on the top of the four mules they brought with them to be sold on the way.

'Thank you, ladies.' Vilson lifted his hat from his head. 'Your help is very much appreciated,' he said giving them some large pieces of beef to take home as a thank-you gift.

Late afternoon, Branquinha, Murilo and the girls were sitting on the salon when they saw Vilson stepping in the porch.

'Hello, Vilson!' Pequena said, climbing down from the table she was sitting on. 'I thought you would be too busy to be coming back here to see Bran... Lucinda!'

'Pequena!' Branquinha and Murilo spoke at the same time.

'You are right, Pequena. It was a busy and tough day, but we have just finished it and I thought I would invite Lucinda to come and go for a boat ride down the river with me.'

'Can I come too?' Pequena moved towards Branquinha, ready to leave.

'No!' Murilo replied. 'They don't need a gooseberry!'

Vilson had borrowed a small boat from the butcher. 'I have always loved water!' he shouted over the roaring of the small engine.

They drove up the river for about ten minutes and found a spot of white sand. Vilson manoeuvred the boat to a shallow part of the water near the edge and they got off the dinghy.

Vilson took his clothes off and dove into the water inviting her with him.

'Are you not scared of caimans?' Branquinha tiptoed her foot into the water, still with her clothes on.

'It's too early for them to be out. Besides the trepidation of the engine on the water will have scared them for an hour or so.'

The water dripping from Vilson's body reminded Branquinha of a TV advertisement she had seen when she was young.

'Come on!' Vilson invited Branquinha again.

Vilson sat on the sand, his back leaning against a stone and with Branquinha resting against his chest. 'The sun will set over there.' Vilson pointed to where the River Jamanxim bent, its water swirling faster. 'It is in moments like this that I love my job the most,' he said.

'A-woman-in-each-port type of guy then!' Branquinha joked, turning her head around towards him and laughing.

'You know what I mean,' he said kissing her ear. 'I love the sunsets. Most late afternoons when we find a place to camp, I look for a secluded spot, away from the men, so I can watch the sky as the sun goes down on the horizon. There are very few things that touch me more than the colours behind the clouds at this time of the day.'

Branquinha didn't say anything. She knew that was a special moment and words would only spoil what she was feeling, so instead of speaking, Branquinha held his arms closer around her and they stayed there until the sun had been swallowed by the river.

Leave Bitterness Behind

It was early morning and Branquinha could not sleep. The thin wood partitions did not stop the noises coming from the outside world and she could hear the snoring of the customers in the other rooms. Usually, Branquinha loved the faded noise of the river flowing not far beneath and the loud birds chirping on the trees nearby, but today all she could sense was the nauseous smell of the dead cows' carcasses that the river had not taken away.

She was glad the overnight customer had preferred to sleep in a hammock instead of on a mattress. She looked at the green polyester fabric of the hammock crossing the room, hanging on the metal hooks nailed on the wall, and thanked the heavens above that half of her overnight clients liked sleeping that way.

She could see the shape of his head turned towards her, but it was too dark for her to see his face. She closed her eyes and tried to recall what he looked like, but she couldn't and instead she remembered the face of the merchant from the first night. Her stomach turned.

Vilson had left the week before and she missed him. Having to be with other men had become even more difficult after meeting Vilson.

Branquinha moved towards the edge of the bed, but as her customer rolled over in his hammock and stopped snoring, she froze. *If he wakes up, he will want more*, she thought. She stayed in the same position for a while staring at the walls and watching the light slowly coming in through the tiny gaps in the wooden wall.

Branquinha compared it with her place back home. Once upon a time they lived in town, but when her father left, her mother was forced to sell the house and move to a smallholding on the outskirts.

It was a shabby and desolate piece of land but, when they moved in, her mother had planted lots of guava and mango trees and as they grew taller the birds started coming. Branquinha loved birds and butterflies and she loved the large watermelons that their small field produced.

Branquinha breathed in and covered her eyes, holding back her tears. It would not be long until she would be able to go home. She hoped the money she had sent would be enough to pay for the first consultation with the cardiologist and the expensive tests her mother needed.

Branquinha and her mum were good friends. Not having any family nearby had brought them close to one another. Branquinha worried about leaving her mother all by herself for so long.

A few more months and she would have enough money to pay for all the medical treatment her mother needed and she would be able to go back home; to escape the clients and the shame that the place gave her.

Branquinha had had a lot of clients since arriving at Casa da Branca. Men paid well for fresh meat...

The thought made Branquinha feel cheap and humiliated. She tried to think of something else.

'Leave bitterness behind.' Branquinha remembered her mother's advice.

Branquinha's thoughts went back to the birds at home. She thought about the sunshine and blue skies. Branquinha missed all these things but most of all she missed her mum's hugs.

The Motorbike

Carmem, Branquinha and Pequena were sitting on the porch, talking to Seu Mineiro, the black, tall and slim gentleman who had an allotment half a kilometre up the road and sold fruit and vegetables in the morning and fruit salad in the afternoons when they heard a motorbike making some weird noises up the road.

'A new driver,' Carmem laughed. 'People shouldn't buy a car before they learn to drive.'

'But then how do they learn if they don't practise?' Pequena asked.

The motorbike roared nearer and stalled. Branquinha leaned over the banister. 'Is that Murilo?'

'Murilo? You're joking?' Carmem jumped off her chair and walked down the steps, followed by Pequena.

'It's him.' Pequena burst into laughter, pointing at Murilo up the road. The bartender tried to avoid one of the larger ditches on the road, swirled across and almost hit a car parked outside Dijé's restaurant.

Dona Branca and the other girls, hearing them laughing, came out of the salon. 'What's he doing with that motorbike?' Zulmira asked when she noticed Murilo was driving it. 'The mad boy is going to hurt himself!'

They all stood there watching Murilo attempting to start the engine and eventually succeeding. As he came down the road, the red shiny bike started gaining speed and, as he manoeuvred it towards them, it became clear to them that Murilo did not know where the brakes were.

'He's going towards the river,' Dona Branca shouted. 'Someone stop him!'

As Murilo came past them, Branquinha grabbed the back rail of the bike and held it. It slowed down a little, but Branquinha wasn't heavy enough to stop it. Pequena joined in and held the back of the bike too.

'Help! I can't stop it!' Murilo shouted to a group of miners standing near Seu Leonardo's kiosk.

The men didn't move fast enough. Murilo, in desperation to avoid the river, twisted the handlebar of the bike so suddenly that he lost control and Branquinha, Pequena, Murilo and the bike ended up on the ground with a huge crowd gathered around them laughing.

For days, Murilo was teased about his driving skills, but he didn't give up learning to drive his new motorbike and a week later he was a professional at driving his bike on the uneven roads around Jardim do Ouro.

The First Letter

'Branquinha! Branquinha!' Murilo screamed from the salon, his voice echoing through the corridor. 'There was a letter for you in the money bag at the gold trading shop. I can see from the sender details at the back that it's from your mother.'

Branquinha threw her book on the pillow and ran to the salon.

It was her mother's first letter since she had arrived in Jardim do Ouro.

Gloria de Dourados, 21st July.

My darling daughter

I have just received your letter and I am sorry you are so concerned. You should not worry about my wellbeing, love, because the money you sent was more than enough to pay for the consultation with the cardiologist and all the tests. I didn't have to spend any money on medication, you see. The doctor, a wonderful woman called Paula, had a lot of samples and she gave me enough to keep me going for a whole month.

The pastor came round the other day and fixed the leaking roof. The hole got bigger and I had water pouring right on top of the stove. It is a relief to not to have to worry about getting the wood wet or the fire dying out half way through cooking dinner. His wife brought lots of clothes to mend and I can do that work while sitting down so I have enough money for the rest of the month. I'm still doing the laundry for the de Souza Family but now I don't need to deliver any more, because they agreed to come to collect it.

Also, the watermelons have been selling well. Lucas, the neighbour's son is coming to help me every morning before going to school and I made enough money to buy beans, rice, oil and sugar for two months. You would love to be here now. The mango and cashew trees are covered in flowers and this year we will have enough fruit to make plenty of mango jam to sell.

I'm so pleased to hear you are enjoying your job at the hotel. The other chambermaids sound like good girls and I'm glad you like Zulmira's cooking. You have always been so fussy with your food.

You have no idea how relieved I am to hear that where you live there is no malaria. Are you sure you can't catch it from the hotel guests who have it?

Please do not worry any more about me. I'm recovering well and soon I will be able to go back to do more laundry.

I miss you terribly, though, and can't wait for you to come back home.
With all my love
Mum

Branquinha stared at the letter, a tear dropping on the page and seeping through to the paper underneath.

'Is your mum all right?' Murilo asked.

Branquinha nodded. 'She's fine, but she must be working so much harder now that I'm not there. There is no running water in our house and we have to get water from the well in the back yard and that is such heavy and hard work.'

Murilo sat next to Branquinha, but could not say anything.

'The watermelons are huge and she has to carry them in,' Branquinha sobbed. 'That is not work for an old woman with heart problems.'

'You will soon go home, Branquinha.'

'Murilo, "go home"?' She lifted her face to Murilo, her eyes puffed and her nose red. 'No one wants to be here; no one wants this life, but nobody ever goes home! People come here because they get paid ten times more than anywhere else in the country, yet most can't save enough to go back.'

Murilo didn't say anything, for he knew Branquinha was right.

'I have no job, no profession.' She leant her head on the table, and continued, sobbing, 'All I'm good for is to open my legs and let the men in.'

'Just keep going, sister.' Murilo sat on the table. 'You soon will be going back and you'll be able to help her.'

'Keep going where to, Murilo?' Branquinha sniffed. 'If I go home now, what will happen next time my mother needs the doctor?'

'I know it's hard, but sometimes it works. You need a plan, sister. You need something to focus on; something that will keep you going and will change your future.'

Murilo and Branquinha spent the rest of the afternoon talking about possible plans and eventually they decided that Branquinha didn't need a lot of money. Her mother owned the small shack and land where they lived and if she saved enough, they could build a large kitchen garden and have a chicken farm. The land was big enough for that.

'Thank you, Murilo. You're a very good friend.' Branquinha hugged Murilo.

'Don't thank me; they were all your ideas.' Murilo hugged Branquinha back.

'What's going on with all this hugging?' Zulmira came into the room with Pequena.

Murilo leaned forward and, waving his arms around, he said, 'Zulmira, Pequena, let me introduce you to Dona Lucinda, Brazil's future Chicken Queen!'

The Pedlar

Murilo rushed into Branquinha's bedroom. 'Can I borrow some money, please?'

'Again, Murilo?' Branquinha twisted her mouth in disapproval.

'You get money every day and I only get paid on Fridays.'

'You know I'm sending money to my mum on Friday.'

'I will pay you in the morning, before you send the money.'

Branquinha sighed. 'What is it for, this time? Something for Serginho, by any chance?'

'There's a new pedlar in town and I saw a shirt I want to buy for him.' There was a pause while he waited for Branquinha to reply. 'Please...'

'A pedlar?' Branquinha asked. It was rare that a pedlar came to the village. Jardim do Ouro was too far from anywhere and most sales people thought the trip to a remote village in the middle of the Amazon rain forest and all its dangers was not worth the money.

'Yeah, she's is having lunch at Dijé's but she'll come here after she's finished. Maybe you could get a few things from the pedlar to make you more...' Murilo took a second before he completed his sentence, '... beautiful.'

'I can't afford clothes right now.'

Murilo cupped Branquinha's face with his right hand. 'You need to look your best to make more money.'

Branquinha didn't reply.

'I'll go and wake the other girls up.' Murilo walked to the door and turned round. 'I take it you're lending me the money, then,' he said, and laughed, running off down the corridor.

'This boyfriend of yours is going to bankrupt you before long...'

Branquinha shouted but not sure if Murilo could hear her.

The tables in the salon were covered with clothes. There were dresses of all colours, jeans, bright tops, shoes, handbags and everything a woman needs to impress her customers, and more.

'Have you got any nail polish?' Carmem went straight to the box of cosmetics which the pedlar had placed on a side table.

'Yes, yes, I have everything... help yourself to my things and make yourselves beautiful.' The pedlar stretched her arms open to her goods lying on the tables.

'Dona Filomena, how much for this?' Pequena put the black pencil dress in front of her.

'Daughter, call me Filó or I shall charge you double,' the short lady replied.

'You can't buy that, Pequena. You are not old enough to wear that,' Murilo said, pulling the black dress from Pequena's hand, 'Try this one.' He passed her a white dress.

'This dress is too big for her, Murilo.' Carmem took the white dress from Pequena's hands. 'Try these jeans and that red top over there instead.' She pointed to a neglected T-shirt on a pile on a chair. 'It is a beautiful top, but it doesn't fit anyone else.'

'No. I want that dress.' Pequena snapped the black dress from Murilo's hands. 'I am old enough to choose my own clothes!'

'You'll look like a...' Murilo started.

'Don't, Murilo!' Branquinha shouted.

'Let him say it, and I'll tell Martinho next time he is here.' Pequena had tears in her eyes.

'I was going to say... uhm... black will make you look even smaller,' Murilo concluded, unconvincingly.

'That was not what you were going to say...'

'Come on, Pequena. Let's try it on and you can decide for yourself.' Branquinha scolded Murilo.

'And take the jeans,' Carmem suggested.

'I'll try the jeans if Branquinha tries the white dress.'

'I'm not buying anything,' Branquinha said, firmly. 'I'm sending money to my mum on Friday and I really can't afford anything.'

'Daughter, I won't charge you to try it on.' Filó put the white dress in Branquinha's hand.

When she walked back in the room wearing the white dress everyone went quiet for a few seconds.

'Oh, Our Lady in Heaven!' Dona Filó opened her arms. 'Daughter, you look like an angel.'

'You must buy it,' someone said. 'You look so beautiful.'

'Yes Branquinha, buy it... buy it... buy it...'

'I really can't.' Branquinha went back to her room and took the dress off.

'If you'd not slept with that poor cowboy for three nights in a row without any pay you'd have enough to buy the dress and send money to your mother,' Cloé said coming in and snapped the white dress from Branquinha's fingers.

A few minutes later she brought the dress back and put it back on the pile of clothes. 'I am going away at the end of the month for the winter months and I can buy better things cheaper down south.'

'I bet the white dress didn't fit her like it fitted you,' Carmem whispered to Branquinha. 'Look what I bought, people!' Carmem showed everyone her new red dress. 'Perfect for my singing nights.'

Pequena was persuaded to buy the jeans and red top and she decided that Murilo was right in the end. The dress did make her look smaller.

The women from other brothels came along and, little by little, the clothes disappeared from the table and so did the white dress. By the end of the afternoon, the pedlar had only a couple of small bags left.

Before she left, she knocked on Branquinha's door.

'I bought the white dress six months ago and although lots of women liked it, it was never quite right for anyone,' the pedlar said. 'Daughter, you looked like an angel wearing the dress and you brought me luck. I sold almost all of my stock in one afternoon; it usually takes me ten days.'

'It wasn't me, Filó. You had beautiful things to sell.'

'Daughter, I want you to have this!' And Filó put the folded white dress into Branquinha's hands.

Goodbye for Now

A week later, Vilson came back and stayed only one night, and it wasn't long enough for her to quench the longing she felt for him. Branquinha knew she had finally fallen in love.

'The government has given me a smallholding not far from here, up the road. It is only twelve kilometres away,' Vilson told her. 'Part of the forest has already been cleared from trees. I'll plant the right type of grass and soon the cattle will be able to feed from it.'

Branquinha hugged Vilson closer. 'I'll miss you.'

'I'll be back after the rainy season when the roads are passable.'

'In six months' time...' Branquinha wanted to say more, but she didn't feel she had the right.

Vilson smiled. 'No, it'll be long before that.' He lifted her chin before kissing her lips. 'And when I come back I want you all to myself.'

Branquinha didn't reply.

'How do you fancy living in a ranch?' He kissed her again.

'What do you mean?' Branquinha leaned back and looked in his eyes.

'You know what I mean. I really like you, Lucinda, and I want to take you away from this life.' Vilson held her hands. 'We'll talk when I come back.'

'I'll be here.' She tried not to cry.

They kissed again.

He put his hat on and walked down the steps to the road.

Branquinha leaned against the banister, holding back the tears and with her lips forced into a smile that didn't exist, waving goodbye.

Branquinha was daydreaming about marrying Vilson, being a rancher's wife and a mother.

'Why did you ask me for advice when the first cock that appears in front of you changes your plans?' Murilo didn't measure his words when he was angry. 'Women are stupid and weak. You should be the owner of your own life, not let a man tell you what to do!'

'This is different, Murilo,' Branquinha argued back.

'Different how, Branquinha?' Murilo hit the table with the damp white cloth, wiping it with one stroke. 'What do you know about this cowboy?'

'He is romantic, he treats me well and he loves me...'

'Branquinha, grow up!' Murilo shouted. 'What has this guy done to prove he is serious?'

'I need to give him a chance!' Branquinha stood up to Murilo. 'He is a wonderful man... the man any woman dreams to find and if I don't give him a chance, I will never know what it would be like.'

'Why I waste my time with these stupid whores is beyond me!' Murilo threw the wipe on the counter and disappeared in the corridor at the back.

'You should not get your hopes up, *guapa*,' Carmem said, painting her thumbnail for the tenth time. 'He might not come back.'

'Of course he'll come back!' Pequena said. 'He wants to marry her.'

'Did he ask you to marry him then?' Carmem asked Branquinha.

'He didn't actually ask the big question but he was just short of it.' Pequena turned to Branquinha. 'What did he say again?'

Branquinha moved in the chair, smiling. 'He said he wants to take me away from this life.'

'You see, he basically asked her to marry him.' Pequena looked at Carmem and gesticulated towards Branquinha. 'He will make her happy.'

'Let's hope so, *guapa*, let's hope so.' Carmem carried on painting her nails. 'But in any case,' she stopped and looked at Branquinha, 'it is better to regret things you did than to cry over the things you didn't have the courage to do.'

The Fire

Branquinha sat up in bed, her eyes wide open, but with her head still full of the smoke and shouting of her dreams.

'Fire! There's a fire coming this way! Fire!' someone shouted and Branquinha realised that she was not dreaming.

She reached for the torch under her pillow and jumped out of bed. 'Wake up! Wake up! Fire!' Branquinha couldn't remember the name of the man lying on the hammock above her bed. 'Wake up!'

She put her jeans and a T-shirt on. 'Get up, there is a fire up the road! It's coming down this way!' She reached under the bed for the box containing all her documents and precious mementos. She flashed the torch on the customer's face, but he continued snoring as if the world around him was not about to end.

'Branquinha, Branquinha, get out now!' Murilo shouted from the corridor. 'The fire will be here soon!'

Branquinha opened the door of the room. She could smell the smoke coming through the building. 'Please wake up!' Branquinha screamed. 'Oh my god!' She was crying. 'He doesn't wake up.'

'Get out of here now!' Murilo pushed her out of the way and, grabbing the chamber-pot from the corner, poured the contents on the man's head.

'What the hell...?' The man sat up wiping his face from the night's wee.

'There's a fire! You need to get out now.' Murilo shouted at the man while dragging Branquinha out of the room through the corridor and bumping into people wanting to get out.

'Where is Pequena?' Branquinha shouted.

'She's gone out with Carmem.' Murilo pushed past Branquinha.

'Someone help me with this box!' Branquinha heard Dona Branca shouting and when she pointed the torch towards the back she saw Dona Branca trying to move a wooden chest out of her room.

'We don't have time for that, Branca,' they heard João Preto shouting.

'Help me here, Murilo! Help, Branquinha!' Dona Branca seemed oblivious to the smoke and the cracking noise of the building burning two doors up the road.

'Branca, we must leave it.' João Preto pulled her away from the box. 'You stay here another minute and we will be burnt alive!'

'I'm not leaving without my box!'

'She is going hysterical, João.' Murilo knew only too well that what Dona Branca wanted Dona Branca would get, fire or no fire.

'For God's sake, woman! Do you want to kill all of us?' With Murilo's help, João Preto lifted the chest on his shoulder and walked down the corridor banging the side of the chest on the wooden walls.

They were the last ones to leave. As they crossed the salon towards the outside porch they could see the light coming from the fire in the shop next door.

They gathered across the road, outside Dijé's restaurant, watching the fire eating the wooden building.

'Our Lord, all my stock is gone. My livelihood...' the shop owner cried.

'Why is no one trying to stop the fire?' Carmem asked Murilo. 'We can get water from the river...'

'Don't be stupid.' Murilo snapped at Carmem.

'We can't stand here without trying to do something...' Carmem insisted.

'We had a long summer and not had a drop of rain for three weeks now,' João Preto explained untouched by it. 'The wood in these buildings is like firewood. All we can do is to keep safe.'

For a while they watched the fire from across the road as if they were in front of a mere bonfire, the light from the flames climbing up the building brightening the entire village.

'Our Lady in Heaven!' Branquinha saw Zulmira running down the road, with Seu Antonio, her partner. 'Is anyone hurt?' She was crying. 'Where is Pequena?'

'We're all fine, Zulmira. We had plenty of time to get everyone out.' Pequena seemed to be taking part in an adventure. 'I've got Beatriz and Clarice with me.' She showed the dolls to Zulmira.

The heat from the fire become more intense as it reached the building next door. They could see the trees in the background.

'What if the forest catches fire?' Pequena asked Branquinha.

'I don't know, Pequena.' Branquinha held Pequena's hand close as they moved further away from the fire. 'We are safe here as we are near the river. We can always go into the water and the fire won't go past the buildings of the river bank.'

'Where are we going to go if the fire burns our home?' Pequena looked up to Branquinha.

'Don't worry about it, Pequena.' Carmem came to Branquinha's rescue. 'You are our sister. You can come with me and Branquinha to wherever we go.'

They heard Dona Branca crying. 'I forgot my new bedspread!' Dona Branca began to run back to the building.

'You're crazy, Branca!' João Preto held Dona Branca from behind.

'Let me go.' Dona Branca kicked back at João Preto's leg. 'Let me go.' She screamed to the top of her voice, but João Preto held her from behind and she couldn't move.

The tongues of fire starting leaping up the walls of the Casa da Branca and people knew it would be just a matter of minutes until the house was swallowed by the fire.

'Oh my god, all these years.' Dona Branca dropped to the floor 'All these years to see my house burning down like this!' With only a narrow gap between the buildings they knew it wouldn't be long before the building was gone.

Branquinha knelt on the floor and hugged Dona Branca.

'Mother of God!' Branquinha heard Zulmira's cry at the same time as she felt the heavy rain on her face.

Dijé opened the doors her restaurant and everyone ran for cover inside. Branquinha had never seen rain like that. In a matter of five minutes the fire had gone.

'It's God's work.' Zulmira put her hands together and prayed.

'Our Lady in Heaven...' Dona Branca joined Zulmira in her

thanksgiving.

João Preto and a few other men went back into the Casa da Branca to check if it was safe to go back in. Someone turned the generator on.

'You were in luck, Branca.' João Preto came out of the house. 'There seems to be no damage to the building at all. Just some mild black marks on the left wall but nothing needs replacing.'

Branquinha moved her hair to one side and squeezed the rain water out of it. Holding her box she went inside. She was relieved that she hadn't lost all her clothes and her mother's Bible she had left behind.

She walked towards her bedroom praying that her customer would not come back. As she opened the door the strong smell of urine hit her nostrils. She switched the lights on.

Her client was lying in his hammock still fast asleep.

The Gypsy

Sandra Rosa Magdalena, the gypsy, arrived the day after the fire. She is beautiful, Branquinha thought, looking at Sandra Rosa's long jet black hair and her dark olive skin.

'She knew there'd be trouble,' Murilo whispered to Branquinha.

'I wish she'd read my fortune this time.' Pequena crossed her arms.

'You're too young.' Murilo tapped Pequena on the shoulder. 'Next year you'll be fifteen and she will do it then.'

Murilo and Carmem moved a table to a far corner so everyone could have their lives exposed with some privacy.

From the other side of the room Ana and Branquinha watched Sandra Rosa Magdalena preparing for the readings. She covered the square table with a floor-length emerald green satin cloth and placed a bright blue runner on top of it and across the table.

On the middle of the runner Sandra Rosa placed a gold dagger engraved with amber and purple stones and on the right, a gold candle holder with a thin and tall white candle.

'Is she any good?' Branquinha asked Ana discreetly.

Ana nodded. 'Last year she told me to keep away from the river and she was right. I didn't listen to her and went for a boat ride and the boat overturned, drowning my friend Pernambuco. I didn't drown by the grace of Our Lady.' Ana blessed herself with the cross. 'I hope this time she tells me good things.'

Sandra Rosa clicked her fingers and Murilo brought her the carafe of water she had asked him to get for the reading. She poured some into a tall glass goblet and, sitting down, she shut her eyes.

'She's chanting to Saint Sara, the protector of the Gypsies.' Carmem whispered to Branquinha when Sandra Rosa began to rock her head back and forwards chanting a calling song.

Sandra Rosa Madalena's long eyelashes flicked ever so gently, almost as if they were dancing to the chanting.

'You!'

Branquinha jumped from her seat and stared at Sandra Rosa's long red-nailed finger pointing at her.

'Me?' Branquinha placed her open hand against her chest.

'Go on!' Carmem pushed Branquinha gently on the shoulder.

'It is you,' Murilo whispered at the same time.

Branquinha slowly crossed the room and sat on the chair, her hands resting on her lap, her legs disappearing under the green table cloth.

'You're not made for this place. You must leave here before your next birthday.' Sandra Rosa spoke as if she recited a passage of a book.

'But...'

'If you don't leave before July, your mother might not see her daughter alive again.'

'My...' Branquinha started saying, wondering how Sandra Rosa knew her birthday was in July. No one else in the village had known. Her birthday had come and gone with nobody knowing about it.

'Your mother will be fine. She saw the nice lady doctor again last week and she will get better with the medication.' Sandra Rosa didn't pause. 'Write to her today and tell her to drink avocado leaf tea and a spoon of olive oil every morning. That should cure her gallstones.'

'How...'

'I see a good man helping you.'

Branquinha thought of Vilson.

Sandra Rosa took a deep breath and stared into Branquinha eyes. 'Tonight, you must light a red candle and bathe yourself with the petals of seven white flowers, a small twig of an orange tree and a spoon of honey. If you do it for seven nights you will free yourself of all the bad luck you've had...' Sandra Rosa didn't complete her sentence. Instead she started chanting again, with her head waving back and forwards, back and forwards, and her eyes wide open.

Branquinha got up slowly from her chair wondering if she had really just met a woman with different colour eyes: one green, one blue.

The Teacher

The rainy season arrived. First there were heavy showers every day and then just rain, day after day, most of the day, the trees welcoming the long wet kisses of the storms and the soil not dry enough to absorb all the water pouring on its back. The River Jamanxim started rising and each week the ferry was marooned further up the riverbank.

A few miners were lucky enough to mine in drier areas, but others weren't so lucky and people left every day. For Branquinha the days passed slowly and the nights were even more difficult than before she met Vilson almost a month ago.

'When I miss Martinho, my xodó, I put a pillow on my back and hug myself,' Pequena told Branquinha.

Branquinha giggled. 'Is that why sometimes we hear you talking to yourself at night?'

'Yeah. You should try that. It's like he's hugging me and if I talk to him it feels real!'

Branquinha didn't reply.

Without saying anything, Pequena left the room and returned with her sewing-bag. 'Why don't you teach me some more crochet today?'

'Sounds like a good idea, Pequena,' Branquinha said.

'I want to finish the table runner for my mum, and then I'll carry on making my dowry,' Pequena announced. 'I'm going to order some white cotton and make a tablecloth for my house and after that I'll make a bedspread and maybe even a rug.'

'What do you want a bedspread for, silly girl.' Murilo came into the room laughing. 'When you marry Martinho, you'll sleep in a hammock.'

'I won't sleep in a hammock forever!' Pequena undid one of the stitches. 'One day, Martinho will buy a nice house for us and we'll have a proper bed.'

'Is that where you are going to use the rug then? Because at the moment, the only place he has is a bare soil spot in João Preto's shack.' Murilo laughed. 'You should learn to read and write before you learn to crochet.'

'Murilo, why are you doing this to the girl? Leave her alone!'

'Don't worry, Branquinha.' Pequena moved the metal crochet needle quite fast against the orange cotton. 'Murilo is jealous because I have Martinho and you have the cowboy. And in any case, Murilo's grumpy today because Serginho didn't come to see him last night.'

'Oh child, leave me alone!' Murilo left the room, banging the door behind him.

'Is it true that you can't read or write?' Branquinha asked Pequena a few minutes later.

'I can write my name!' Pequena bent her head slightly. 'I went to school for four months when I was eight, but I wasn't clever so my father said I was wasting my time and I had to leave.'

'I could teach you to read and write,' Branquinha offered.

'Could you?' Pequena threw the needle and cotton into the sewing bag lying on the table. 'I have a notebook and pencil.' She ran up to her room.

Branquinha smiled. She would enjoy teaching Pequena to read and write.

Two Letters

'There were two letters in the bank bag for us today. And guess who they are both for?' Carmem said from the door of the salon, waving two envelopes at Branquinha. 'How come in all the time I have lived here, I never got any letters at all?'

'How many did you write this year?' Murilo asked Carmem while mopping the floor. 'Branquinha, read the letters later, please. If I don't wash the floor before Dona Branca gets back she's going to be so annoyed with me.'

'You should have got up early instead of spending most of the morning on hanky-panky with Serginho,' Carmem said passing the letters to Branquinha.

'Oh my god, it's from Vilson!' Branquinha said, rushing to open one of the envelopes.

Loanda, 12th October

My dear Lucinda,

I have no words to tell you just how much I miss you and long to be with you. These feelings are not something I'm familiar with and they are unsettling, but yet I welcome them.

I arrived back in my town the day before yesterday and have started preparing to move to our smallholding in Jardim do Ouro.

My father is away at the moment. He is not well and went away to the city see a doctor. Once he gets back, I will ask him for part of my inheritance in advance and since he has given both of my brothers their share, I am sure he will give me mine too. Things will be a lot easier then. With more money, I can buy a tractor and some of the equipment we will need to use on the land. The first thing we shall do is to fence the spot where we will build our home. The house won't be very big to start with but we will build it in such way that we can expand it as the children come along. Do you think your mother will leave her town to come and live with us? It is a very remote place, but she will be most welcome.

Branquinha read the sentence sobbing.

'Why are you crying, you silly girl?' Murilo hugged Branquinha. 'It is all good, is it not?'

'I know...' Branquinha sniffed and carried on reading.

I have to go now. I agreed to take my mother to have lunch with her best friend. I'm not looking forward to it because last time I was there, about ten years ago, I spilt my dinner plate on my lap trying to cut some meat and the little brat girl and her brothers teased me the entire afternoon.

Will write more at the weekend once I speak to my father.

Missing you and with all my love,

V.

'He's serious then,' Carmem said. 'You deserve to find love, Branquinha. You're a good girl and not born for this life.'

'Nobody's born for this life, Carmem!' Murilo said, going back to washing the floor.

'Carmem said you got two letters from Vilson, today?' Zulmira turned the bread dough around, stretching it. 'He is keen, isn't he?'

'It was only one from Vilson. The other was from my mum.'

'Oh, how is she?' Zulmira stopped kneading the dough and looked at Branquinha.

'Her health is better, but I think she's feeling very lonely.' Branquinha shifted on her chair, her discomfort clear to Zulmira.

'Can't she get someone to come and live with her?' Zulmira suggested.

'Not really. I'm sending her more money this week and I'll suggest she goes to see her sister who lives in São Paulo. She hasn't seen them for over eight years.'

'That is a long time to not see her sister,' Zulmira said.

'I know, but we've been very poor since my dad left and my aunt's in the same situation. The only thing they can afford is letters and exchanging a few photographs over the years,' Branquinha explained. 'This has been the first time we've had money to spare.'

'And what about Vilson then?' Zulmira started rolling the dough into a loaf. 'Carmem said he wants to bring your mum to live with you on his farm.'

'Yes...' Branquinha's cheeks blushed. 'I'm worried about it.'

'Why is that?'

'My mum will find out.'

'It is unlikely. You will live away from the village and she would be isolated from gossip like this.'

'You do realise that my reputation will always follow me, don't you?'

'Branquinha, you can't change your past and you are who you are. When you learn to live with your own ghosts you will live a happier life.'

Gringo

When Murilo saw the blond man walking through the doors, he knew he wasn't about to have another easy Monday.

'Good evening, Gringo.' Murilo had hoped the foreigner wouldn't come until the following week when Cloé would be back. Murilo knew Cloé was very possessive and since Gringo was her most generous client, Murilo also knew she would not be pleased that someone else was benefiting from Gringo's kindness.

'How are things in your mines?' Murilo placed a bottle of Chivas Regal on the table hoping his best whisky – bought specially for Gringo – would make things easier for him.

'The heavy rain has started slowing us down.' Gringo sipped his drink. 'Is Cloé with a client?' he asked.

'She's still away. She'll be back in a few days.'

Gringo lit a cigarette. 'How about the Paraguayan girl?' he asked.

Murilo felt his chances of getting Gringo to come back another day were diminishing by the second.

'Carmem's not available tonight.' Murilo's mind immediately went to the day when Cloé slapped one of the girls in the face for sleeping with one of her customers while Cloé was busy with another. 'I'll see who else can be with you this evening.'

Everyone was worried about upsetting Cloé but Murilo worried more than others because he knew just how much money Cloé brought to the house. He dashed to the back of the house to speak to Dona Branca.

'I told Cloé not take too long or her clients will move on to other women,' Dona Branca said. 'Tell Branquinha to go and sit with him.'

'Branquinha? She's not his type, surely.'

'Exactly! Hopefully he'll try her once and leave her alone next time so Cloé won't lose him.'

'Ah...!' said Murilo. One thing Murilo knew about men was that they tended to favour a certain type of woman and only rarely changed their taste.

Branquinha sat on her chair wearing her white dress, curious, as she watched the man in front of her singing and drumming his fingers on the table to the pace of the foreign song playing on the stereo.

'What does it say?' Branquinha smiled at Gringo hoping he would talk to her.

'What does what say?' Gringo blew his cigarette smoke from the right corner of his mouth.

'What does the song say?'

'It says *I want to break free*,' Gringo translated, drinking the last of his whisky in one go.

Before he could say anything Branquinha poured him some more whisky. 'And what do you want to break free from?'

Gringo went quiet for a minute, puffed his cigarette, slowly sipping his drink. When he finished it, Branquinha poured some more of the gold liquid into the glass and handed it to him. 'You still haven't answered my question. Who or what do you want to break free from?'

Gringo took his glass and swallowed its contents in one go. 'I am free.'

Branquinha sipped her soft drink.

'I've never met anyone who's really free,' Branquinha replied. 'I've met people who are free to do things they want to, but even then, they are not free of their own demons.'

Gringo narrowed his blue eyes and looked at Branquinha's pale and delicate face. He pressed the stub of his cigarette against the metal of the ashtray. 'How old are you?'

'I'm twenty-four.' Branquinha lifted the glass to her lips, bending her head slightly. 'I guess I'm old enough to have my own demons.'

When Gringo looked at her, she smiled.

'Come and dance with me!' Branquinha said, suddenly standing up and pulling Gringo by the hand. 'Dancing is the best weapon of all against demons!'

The following morning, Branquinha's hopes of arriving before Murilo woke up vanished when she saw the water rushing from the salon door and down the street.

'I thought you said you weren't going to wash the floor again until Friday.'

'I told you to not spend the night with Gringo.' Murilo swept the water from the floorboards, banging the brush hard at the front door.

'Well...'

'Well?' Murilo threw the broom against the wall. 'Well?' he shouted with his hands on his hips. 'We'll see when Cloé comes back and finds out you spent the whole night with Gringo at his hotel!'

'She's not here...'

'Oh Branquinha!' Murilo interrupted, going back to sweep the floor. 'Don't pretend you don't know the rules.'

'What rules? He paid for the entire night.'

'Branquinha, you exasperate me!' Murilo threw the brush on the floor, turned around and walked off.

'What does "exasrepate" mean? Pequena said startling Branquinha.

'It is "exasperate", Pequena. It means I drive him mad.'

'Why can't he say that then, instead using all these long words? And why was he exasrepated with you then?'

Branquinha didn't correct Pequena this time. 'He is just looking out for me.'

'It's because you went to sleep in Gringo's hotel, isn't it?' Pequena whispered, grabbing a broom.

'Shush,' Branquinha said putting her finger on her lips. She picked up a brush and started to sweep the water from the room.

'Oh you're back!' Zulmira came into the room. 'Last night, after you left, Dona Branca came looking for you and she went crazy when she found out that you went to Gringo's hotel room.'

'I don't know what the big deal is! He paid enough for five sessions and an overnight.' Branquinha tried to explain her actions.

'It is more than I usually make.'

'The big deal is that you should not have gone with him, you bloody idiot!' Murilo came back into the room and grabbed the broom from Pequena's hand and started sweeping again. 'The big deal is that when Cloé comes back and finds out that you went to his hotel room, you are going to be in so much trouble that you will wish you hadn't been born!' Murilo chucked the bucket of water on the floor, splashing water on everyone.

'I...'

'Did you know that Cloé's never been invited to Gringo's hotel room or spent the whole night with him?' Zulmira asked.

'If Cloé never slept a whole night with Gringo then he's not her xodó then...,' Pequena interrupted.

'Oh well, there's nothing you can do now. Go and have a shower Branquinha,' Zulmira said. 'Come on Pequena, let's go and get those eggs from Seu Didi!'

As Branquinha walked away she heard Murilo shouting, 'Cloé will drink your blood when she gets back, I'm warning you!'

Branquinha spent the rest of the morning tidying her room and clearing her head. She had no intention of keeping Gringo to herself but she envied Cloé. He had treated Branquinha as a person and made her forget that she was being paid for her services.

Branquinha thought about their night together. When they left the house, instead of running to the first bed available, Gringo had invited her to sit by the river and they talked for a long time.

Gringo lit a cigarette and told her how much he loved the forest; the noises that the creatures made in the night, the stars in the sky and the peace that the jungle gives.

'There are so many insects by the river though,' Branquinha had argued.

'You need to ignore them to learn to appreciate its beauty.' He laughed. 'One day I'll take you to the spring near my shack. There are thousands of beautiful butterflies. Some of them are huge and their colours are incredibly bright.'

In the afternoon Dona Branca called for Branquinha. 'You are young, but if you want to last in this business, you must keep away from the other girls' men, Branquinha.'

'I'm sorry, I shouldn't have gone to his hotel but I didn't think...' Branquinha started crying. 'He was so kind to me, Dona Branca.'

'I know, child. I know how you feel. He is a good-looking man and he treats women well, but you mustn't let that get to your head.' Dona Branca unrolled some toilet paper and passed it to Branquinha.

'I'm not going to let him get to my head Dona Branca. You know I love Vilson, the drover,' Branquinha replied, blowing her nose on the toilet paper.

'You must keep away from Gringo, though.'

'What's going to happen when Cloé comes back and finds out?'

'We'll figure something out.' Dona Branca hugged Branquinha. 'Now, go and wash your face and get Murilo over here.'

Branquinha didn't regret sleeping with Gringo but she wished no one else had known about it because now everyone was talking about it and wanted to know more.

'Did you know Cloé killed a man before she came to live here?' Pequena said to Branquinha at the table at lunchtime.

'Pequena, stop talking nonsense! Remember what I told you about not spreading rumours,' Zulmira said.

'It's not a rumour! I heard Cloé telling Carmem.' Pequena looked at Carmem. 'Tell them Carmem, tell them!'

Carmem didn't say anything, but nodded in agreement before eating another mouthful of rice and beans.

'Girls, we must keep quiet about this.' Zulmira stood up and leaned on the table. 'It's the only way we can protect Branquinha.'

'Don't worry, *guapa*.' Carmem put her hand on Branquinha's hand. 'Everything will be OK.'

'Yes, everything will be all right,' Pequena repeated while reaching for another piece of steak.

'What is going to be all right?' They all froze hearing Cloé's voice. 'What have I been missing?'

Zulmira was very quick to answer 'Oh, just bad news about Branquinha's mum.'

'What's wrong with your mother?' Cloé asked Branquinha,

sitting down and helping herself to some salad. 'I thought you said she's getting treatment with the money you've been sending her.'

'Yes...,' Branquinha said, scared.

'Yes, but the doctors want to do more tests.' Zulmira came to the rescue again. 'How was your trip, Cloé dear? You took so long I was beginning to think you'd stay there until Christmas... How are your little girls?' Zulmira pulled the meat dish towards Cloé. 'Did you bring any photos of them?'

That night, just before Carmem started her show, Branquinha saw Cloé heading towards her and she knew that Cloé had found out about her sleeping with Gringo.

'Dona Branca told me that you didn't want to shag Gringo because he was my xodó but she made you do it because business is slow and she is short of money this month.'

Branquinha wasn't quite sure of what was happening, but she kept quiet.

'I'll let you off this time, but you keep away from him,' Cloé added.

Branquinha couldn't speak.

'You make sure you keep away from him.' Cloé repeated and looked at Branquinha, slowly, from top to toe. 'He is mine!'

As Cloé walked away Branquinha breathed out slowly with relief, but thought to herself, *You silly woman. Men like Gringo belong to no one other than themselves!*

All Souls Day

October finished wet. It was almost All Souls Day. The cemetery might have seemed far too big for a small place like Jardim do Ouro but people didn't live long lives in the village.

The large square plot of land, a kilometre and half away from town, was fenced by wooden planks. At the front, the fence was washed with white paint and its large gate opened to a wide path that led to a small wooden chapel in the middle of the graveyard.

'It is amazing how people spend so much money on the dead instead of concentrating on the living ones.' Murilo held the gate open for Branquinha and Pequena.

'Look at that tall mausoleum, for example.' Murilo pointed to a burnt yellow vault standing out against the other colourful graves. 'How much money did they waste on that? Why not give it to someone who needs it now?'

'It was probably someone they loved, Murilo.'

'When we die we all go to the same place, Branquinha,' Murilo replied. 'From the dust you came to the dust I shall take you.'

Pequena stopped and putting the bucket she was carrying on the ground, she asked Murilo, 'If that is the case why are we repainting Ritinha's grave then?'

'Pequena, you should not say that!' Murilo chastised her. 'Ritinha was special.'

Two hours later, Murilo walked around the concrete box raised above the ground and painted in light blue. 'Now, it's perfect!' he said with his hands on his hips.

'I still think we should have painted it in pink.' Pequena disagreed. 'Blue's a boy's colour.'

'Light blue was Ritinha's favourite colour,' Murilo pointed out to Pequena.

'The pink flowers will make it a very girly tomb,' Murilo said, taking a bunch of pink plastic flowers from the bag lying beside him and placing them in the tall red vase which was cemented on the side of the tomb.

'Next year,' Murilo went on, 'when I've enough money, I'll get someone to tile the entire tomb and put a big tall cross. It'll be a proper mausoleum and the most beautiful one in the cemetery.'

'Where's the new photo?' Pequena asked.

'It is not ready yet. Dona Branca got it from the photo shop in Moraes de Almeida yesterday but they're going to put it in a special frame and this afternoon when Zeca do Pagode comes from Mina Dourada, he'll cement it in,' Murilo said.

'Let's go, people!' Branquinha grabbed the brushes and the bucket and started walking towards the gate. 'Zulmira will tell us off if we're late for lunch.'

On their way out, as they passed the 'Cruzeiro', the large cross at the front of the cemetery where people lit candles for those who were buried elsewhere, they saw Dona Branca arriving with a large wreath of pale yellow plastic roses.

'I ordered a white and pink one,' Dona Branca explained, 'but they made a mistake and I had to take the yellow, but actually I'm glad because Ritinha would prefer a brighter colour.'

'Ritinha loved blue. She'd have been happy.' Zulmira poured a ladleful of beans on to Murilo's plate. 'Saint Maria Madalena, the patron saint of the prostitutes, pray for her soul.' Zulmira blessed herself with the sign of the cross.

'Amen!' everyone responded together.

'She'd have been proud of you, Murilo,' Carmem added.

'Don't be stupid!' Cloé said, her mouth still full. 'She is burning in hell as we speak!'

'Cloé!' Carmem and Murilo said almost in unison while Pequena stared at Cloé with her big eyes open wide.

'Don't wish ill to the dead,' Zulmira reprimanded Cloé.

'I'm not *wishing* anything.' Cloé skewered a tomato from the salad plate in the middle of the table. 'Everybody knows where whores end up: burning in hell.'

'They don't!' Pequena protested. 'If they repent before they die, they get a second chance.'

'Eat your food, it's getting cold,' Murilo told Pequena. 'And don't listen to Cloé. She doesn't know anything about going to heaven.'

Cloé was about to answer Murilo when Dona Branca entered the room. She was the only one allowed to have lunch at any time she wanted.

'Zulmira, tomorrow, dinner's at five-thirty. We're opening early for All Souls Day and I don't want a repeat of last year.' Dona Branca sat down at the head of the table near the large terracotta water filter. 'The boys from Mina Dourada will go to the cemetery in the afternoon and will all be here by six, if not earlier. They asked me to buy extra candles for Ritinha.'

'I never knew they were friends with Ritinha. I thought it was just Zeca do Pagode,' Branquinha said.

'Ritinha was friends with everyone, Branquinha,' Zulmira explained. 'She was the kindest girl we ever had in this house.' Zulmira looked towards Cloé as if to warn her to keep her mouth shut. 'When any of the girls were ill she looked after them like they were her sisters.'

'When I had malaria for the first time, I was sure I was going to die, but Ritinha sat with me for hours and hours telling me I would live to tell the story,' Murilo recalled.

'She was so nice, Branquinha.' Pequena leant her head on her arm with her elbow resting on the table. 'Every time she went home she'd bring me a present and last Christmas,' Pequena paused, 'she got me Beatriz, my porcelain doll.' Pequena closed her eyes and two large tears dropped on her face.

'How did she die?' Branquinha asked the girls.

'Ah *guapa*, it was so sad. She was standing outside in the street talking to Seu Didi, waiting for him to make her a kebab, when she was hit by a stray bullet,' Carmem explained. 'She died before we got her to the hospital.'

'Let's eat,' Zulmira said, blowing her nose in a white handkerchief with the letter Z embroidered in orange on a corner. 'The food's getting cold.'

The meal lasted a long time for nobody was hungry.

The following morning most of the girls got up early to go to the cemetery. Everyone knew a person or two who had died while they were there and were buried in the town. Jardim do Ouro was a dangerous place. The miners used to say if someone lived there long enough you would either get murdered or malaria would take care of them anyway.

'How come there's no surname on the plaque?' Branquinha asked Murilo.

Murilo didn't reply. He knelt beside Ritinha's tomb. Taking four thin white candles from the box in his bag, he struck the match, cupping his hand to protect the flame against the wind, and lit the wick of each candle.

'We never knew her surname,' Zulmira said. 'All we knew is that she was called Ritinha and came from a town named Bragantina in the Parana State.' Zulmira bent her head towards Branquinha's ear. 'We only knew her birthday because she was born on the same day as Carmem and they celebrated their birthday together.'

Zulmira, Pequena and Branquinha watched Murilo still kneeling with his eyes closed, praying with his hands together.

'He is praying for her soul in case she died too quickly and didn't have time to repent her sins,' Pequena explained.

People came and left all the day and many candles were lit for Ritinha's soul and placed next to her name in her tomb. Everyone liked the small framed photo that Zeca do Pagode had cemented to the headboard of the tomb.

That evening Murilo didn't come to the kitchen for dinner and in the night he was very quiet. He wiped the surface of the counter with a white cloth and polished the glasses. At the salon he didn't sing along with the songs playing on the stereo.

Carmem didn't feel like doing her Paraguayan Show.

When Zeca do Pagode arrived with his colleagues from Mina Dourada, Murilo was about to retire to his room.

'My friend, Ritinha might have died, but she is not gone,' Zeca do

Pagoda said, tapping Murilo on the back. 'She'll still be alive in our hearts and memories until the day we die.'

'You are right,' Murilo replied.

A few minutes later, Murilo started playing Ritinha's favourite song and Carmem jumped out of her chair to sing.

'This song goes to our wonderful friend Ritinha!' Carmem shouted when she took to the microphone.

Pequena danced with Carmem and soon the miners, Murilo and the girls were all singing happily.

Branquinha watched them, wishing she'd known Ritinha.

Jandaia

Winter was a tough time in Jardim do Ouro. The rain stopped everyone and everything. The river was so flooded the ferry had to use planks of wood to reach the river banks and the water was very close to reaching some of the floorboards underneath the houses.

A lot of people left the region and Casa da Branca closed early most nights.

The new girl arrived late the night before and no one had seen her, and those who had, had not noticed how ugly she really was.

'I don't know where Dona Branca finds these women. This one looks like she had a fight with a bull,' Murilo said.

'She isn't that ugly.' Branquinha knew Murilo was scared of bulls, but even for him that was a harsh comparison.

'Have you seen her eyes? They look like they are about to pop out!' he carried on, 'And what is it with the sunglasses?'

'She probably wears them because she hates her eyes,' Branquinha said.

'And rightly so!' Murilo laughed. 'This morning when I came out of the shower she was waiting outside. I nearly had a heart attack when I saw her staring at me.'

Branquinha didn't reply.

'What about her nose then? It seems to have crashed into a wall and never bounced back!' Murilo pretended to bump into the wall and laughed.

'Murilo! You shouldn't say these things,' Branquinha said, her voice giving away her irritation. 'Surely she has something good in her, everybody does, and if she smartens up a little she'll look a lot better.'

'Smarten up? That one? I'd pay money to see that happening.' Murilo put his fingers together and pointed to his own hair. 'Have you seen her hair? It hasn't seen a pair of scissors in years and I bet she washes it with the same bar of soap she washes her clothes!'

Branquinha moved on the chair, feeling slightly uncomfortable. Murilo had commented a few times on her own lack of effort in making herself looking sexy.

'Shush, she's coming,' Branquinha warned Murilo. 'Good morning, Jandaia. Did you sleep well?'

'Good morning!' Jandaia's voice was soft and warm and her accent was slightly different from everyone else's. 'I heard about the fight last night. Is Carmem all right?'

'She is still in hospital...'

'If you count twelve stitches on the arm as all right!' Murilo interrupted Branquinha. 'She had to have two litres of blood, but she is so lucky because João Preto was here last night and he is a universal donor.'

'What is a universal donor?' Jandaia asked.

'Ugly *and* stupid!' Murilo muttered under his breath, rolling his eyes. 'Universal donor,' Murilo spoke very slowly, as if he was talking to a child, 'is a person with a type of blood called O negative. They can donate blood to almost anyone.'

'Ah!' Jandaia seem impressed with Murilo's knowledge. 'So what was the fight about?' he asked Branquinha.

'Two miners arguing about gold,' Branquinha replied. 'The older miner accused the younger one of stealing gold from their mine while he was away on business. The younger one got very aggressive and punched the older one. Carmem jumped between them trying to stop the fight, but by this time, the older one had pulled a knife and stabbed Carmem by accident.'

'There was blood everywhere,' Murilo told Jandaia. 'It took me hours to wash it clean.'

'Oh...' Jandaia covered her mouth. 'Poor Carmem!'

'She was lucky,' said Branquinha. 'She could easily have been killed.'

'Murilo and I are going to the hospital soon,' Branquinha said to

Jandaia. 'Would you like to come with us?'

When Murilo, Jandaia and Branquinha got to the hospital, Carmem was crying. 'I can't do anything. I can't even paint my own nails. The money I have is not enough to pay the hospital bill.'

'What about that money you're saving to buy that singing club in Paraguay?'

'Ah, *guapa,* I'm including that.' Carmem sobbed again.

When Carmem told them how much the bill was, Murilo and Branquinha almost fell back. It was a small fortune and they knew Carmem would spend many months working to pay it.

'If I had gone to Seu Geraldo's Pharmacy, I would not have ended up with such a big bill.'

'Seu Geraldo and his daughter could have stitched the wound, but you lost a lot of blood,' Murilo explained to Carmem.

'The business is already so quiet because of the rain and now, with my arm like this,' Carmem lifted her arm wrapped in bandages, 'I'll have to give up my job in the ice cream parlour too.'

'I hope you learnt your lesson and don't try to separate men fighting and let them kill themselves.' Murilo blinked slowly and twisted his lower lip as he did when he was upset. 'You should count yourself lucky for still being alive.'

'Concentrate on getting better, Carmem. Things will soon brighten up.' Branquinha sat by Carmem's bed and held her hand.

'I've an idea!' Jandaia said, almost shouting, 'We could organize a party and collect money to help Carmem.'

Murilo rolled his eyes skywards. 'Yeah, that'll help!'

'We could send out a word to all her clients and ask them to contribute. Then we could also get a live band,' Jandaia persisted.

'That will cost more than we'd make in the party,' Murilo said. All the way back home he argued with Jandaia about her plans to help Carmem.

'She's just trying to help,' Branquinha pointed out.

'The road to hell is paved with good intentions,' replied Murilo, walking faster and leaving Jandaia and Branquinha behind.

Help started arriving the following afternoon. When Jandaia went to the hospital to paint Carmem's nails, Carmem told her that one of her clients had come to see her and gave her five grams of gold and also had brought two more grams from someone else.

Carmem left the hospital, but help continued to come in, a little here and a little there.

The day after Carmem left hospital, João Preto turned up and when he heard how much the foreign girl had spent on hospital bills for stopping the men killing each other, he got Sergeant Armando to go and bring the two men into the Police Station.

'Why are we here?' one of the men asked Sergeant Armando. 'We didn't make a formal complaint to the police. There is no need for this!'

'Good morning, gentlemen. I'm João Preto and I understand that the other day you were in my friend Branca's establishment, were you not?'

'You see that girl there?' João Preto pointed to Carmem sitting in a corner, her arm still in bandages. 'I'm not sure if she is the most stupid person I have ever met or the bravest woman in this village.'

The men sat on their chairs, scared, their eyes going from Carmem to each other and then looking down on the floor. They both knew about João Preto's ruthlessness

'I need you to help me to decide,' said João Preto, finally.

'I'm sorry the woman was hurt but it was none of her business, Seu João Preto,' the younger of the men said.

'Her name is Carmem, by the way,' João Preto said.

'Yeah,' the older guy agreed. 'It was men's business which... uhm, Carmem, had nothing to do with.'

'Let me tell you how I see it.' João Preto paused for a few seconds, making everyone uncomfortable. 'I think Carmem,' João Preto paused again, 'saved the life of one of you and kept the other out of prison.' João Preto's voice was low and slow. 'What do you think, Sergeant Armando?'

'I would say it's a fair assessment, sir,' Sergeant Armando replied to João Preto.

'If you look at it like this, I guess so, but she still had no business to butt in,' the younger man answered back, while the older was wise enough to keep his mouth shut.

'So you think she was stupid in getting involved?' João Preto said to the younger man.

The man, believing João Preto was supporting him, said, 'Yeah... I do, sir. I'm sorry she was hurt, but it was none of her business.'

'Thank you for your opinion, young man. In that case,' João Preto turned to Sergeant Armando, 'arrest this man for carrying a knife and disturbing business in my friend's place.'

While Sergeant Armando and his helpers dragged the man into a cell, João Preto spoke to the older man.

'And what do you think? Was she stupid or brave?'

'The girl was brave, very brave, Seu João Preto,' the old man replied, his face pale.

'Do you think she saved your life?' João Preto asked the man.

'Yes, she did, sir. That boy,' he pointed out towards the door, 'was stealing gold from my mine. He could have killed me as well!'

'In that case, you owe this woman some money as compensation for what she had to spend on hospital bills. You are lucky that you have to pay only the hospital bill, because her friends are raising money to cover her time off.'

The miner didn't argue because the price could have been a lot higher.

On the Saturday, the night of the party, Murilo was surprised to see one of the most popular bands in the area, "Los Paraguayos", arriving to play, for free.

Murilo looked at them standing tall on the stage and realised that they didn't look at all bad with their pristine white long-sleeved shirts tucked into pressed black trousers contrasting with the shiny red accordions and mandolins. Now that Carmem had recovered the money for the hospital bills, there was a lot less pressure and everybody seemed more relaxed.

'What's it with the red, white and blue sash?' Jandaia asked one of the members of the band.

'It represents our national flag, *señorita*.'

Dona Branca, who had supported the idea from the beginning, was at the door helping bring customers from the street.

'We'll soon be playing *Galopeira*!' Dona Branca called from the porch, knowing that the most popular Paraguayan song in Brazil would attract the men in. 'Played by a band all the way from Paraguay!' Dona Branca shouted at the top of her voice.

Once the group started playing, passers-by began to pour in and when they heard about the tragedy of the beautiful Paraguayan girl, still with her arm bandaged, sitting in the corner, they couldn't but help.

The dance floor was so full Dona Branca had to stop people coming in and the last customers didn't leave until after three in the morning.

'What a great night!' said Murilo, counting his commission while Branquinha got some water for her overnight client. 'And did you see how much money Carmem made?'

Neither Branquinha nor Murilo heard Jandaia coming into the room. 'You see, Murilo, even an ugly girl has something good about her,' he said before walking away.

Gringo Visits Casa da Branca Again

Murilo was busy fixing the microphone for Carmem's singing and by the time Murilo saw Gringo it was too late. He was already talking to Branquinha.

'I can't see you,' Murilo heard Branquinha saying to Gringo.

'Why not?' Gringo's accent was heavier than usual. 'I thought we got on well.'

'Yes, but I...'

'Because Cloé will kill her if she sees you and Branquinha together,' Murilo interrupted.

'Why would she do that? No offense to Cloé, but she's not exactly my girlfriend, is she?' Gringo asked Murilo, laughing.

'Gringo, I'll go and get you a whisky while you wait for Cloé.' Murilo pulled a chair for Gringo at one of the tables and placed a clean ashtray on the middle of the table. 'She won't take long.'

Murilo grabbed Branquinha's hand and dragged her to the storage room behind the bar. 'What are you thinking? You'll get killed.'

'Murilo, I didn't do anything. It's not my fault that Gringo prefers me to her!'

'It's not your fault but it's your neck that's on the line,' Murilo said. 'Keep away from him!'

When they got back to the salon, Gringo had gone and Murilo was visibly relieved.

'I heard Gringo come in,' said Cloé as she came into the bar a few minutes later, 'Where is he?'

'I don't know,' Murilo said. 'One minute he was here, the next he wasn't.' Murilo washed the two glasses in the sink, avoiding Cloé's gaze. 'He'll probably be back later.'

Not long after that Murilo got an envelope with cash and a note from Hotel das Aguias. *"Please send the girl Branquinha for an overnight"*, the note said.

'You can go but if it's Gringo you must come back immediately,' Murilo warned Branquinha. 'He's trouble for you, sister.'

For the rest of the evening Cloé avoided all customers and Murilo was worried. 'If Dona Branca finds out you're avoiding clients so you can see Gringo if he comes in, she won't be happy.'

'Don't be stupid, Murilo.' Cloé puffed her cigarette smoke out. 'When did you ever see me avoiding clients because I was waiting for a guy?'

Murilo cleared a few glasses and was changing the record when he saw Gringo coming back.

'My liver's not good today. A Coca-Cola, please, Murilo,' said Gringo, tapping his stomach. He was the only customer who ordered anything with the word 'please' and Murilo liked it.

Gringo glanced at Cloé. 'Sorry, beautiful, but I think I've the malaria coming my way so I can't see you tonight.'

'Oh!' Cloé sounded disappointed. 'You can still stay here if you like.'

'I think not, babe.' Gringo drank some of the coke and stood up. 'I'll see you around, yeah?'

The following day when Branquinha came back, Murilo was sitting in the porch.

'Who was it then?' Murilo followed Branquinha as she walked towards her room.

'You don't know him,' Branquinha answered quickly. 'He's someone who owns a dredger down the river.' She moved towards the door.

'You must get him to start coming here because the fees they pay for an outside visit are just about enough to cover the drinks and fees they would spend here.' Money was always the main concern for Murilo.

'I'll try!' Branquinha said.

'Gringo came back last night but didn't stay with Cloé.' Murilo sat on Branquinha's bed. 'She wasn't happy, at all!'

'Oh, did he?' Branquinha opened the door of her room. She leaned over and reached a towel and her washing bag. 'I'm in desperate need of a shower,' she said as she almost ran to the bathroom.

'Sister, come back here, right now!' Murilo shouted.

'What?' Branquinha came back, her face paler.

'Oh my word... it was a plot to fool Cloé!' Murilo stood up and put his hands on his hips. 'You clever little cow.'

'It wasn't my idea, Murilo,' Branquinha whispered. 'When I got there, he told me his plans and I couldn't disagree with him.'

'Branquinha, you're crazy. If anyone finds out what you're doing, you'll be dead meat,' Murilo said walking back to the salon.

Branquinha followed him. 'Please Murilo, don't tell anyone. Please!' she begged.

'Oh, have you got a little secret, have you?' Neither Murilo nor Branquinha heard Cloé coming into the room. 'Murilo, tell Zulmira I'm not coming for lunch. I've decided to play nurse to my xodó today.' Cloé stepped down to the street.

For a while Branquinha stood at the door and watched Cloé's hips waving sideways in her tight pair of red trousers as she walked up the road towards the Hotel das Aguias.

Seu Mineiro

Branquinha, Zulmira, Carmem and Pequena sat on the porch waiting for Seu Mineiro.

'Today is even hotter than yesterday.' Carmem fanned herself for the millionth time. 'How can it be so wet, yet so hot?'

'You are going to break your fan this time,' Zulmira warned Carmem.

'Yeah, and then you won't be able to do your Paraguayan Show,' Pequena reminded Carmem.

'This heat is unbearable; I can't wait to go back to Paraguay,' Carmem complained, waving the fan faster.

'Seu Mineiro is going to be here soon with a fruit salad. Once you have it, you will feel better,' Branquinha said.

Everyone knew the Paraguayan girl had a soft spot for Seu Mineiro.

'Did you know that before Seu Mineiro turns around the corner, he combs his hair and sprays his mouth with mouth freshener?' Pequena said.

Branquinha and Zulmira laughed.

'That is because he likes Carmem,' Branquinha looked at Carmem.

'Why does he never come for you in the nights?' Zulmira asked Carmem.

'He is a Christian believer and he is not allowed to do it outside of the marriage.' Carmem stood up and went to sit on the banister. 'He gave me money to help with the hospital bill, though.'

'Uhm...' Zulmira looked at Carmem.

'He does come in to see me singing from time to time. Then he orders a soft drink and stands in a corner all by himself.'

'Oh...' Branquinha felt sorry for Seu Mineiro.

'There he is!' Pequena shouted.

'Shush!' Branquinha hushed Pequena, 'We don't want him to know we have been talking about him, do we?'

'Fruit salad, freezing cold fruit salad!' Seu Mineiro shouted, parking his muddy cart on the side of the road and was immediately surrounded by lots of people wanting his popular fruit salad. Once the crowd had disappeared, he moved to a spot near Carmem.

'Good afternoon, ladies.'

'Seu Mineiro, it's my birthday tomorrow. Are you going to give me a free fruit like you gave...'

'Pequena!' Zulmira interrupted. 'How many times do I have to tell you that it is rude to ask for presents?'

'Your birthday? That's good.' Neither Pequena nor Seu Mineiro paid attention to Zulmira. 'Are you having a party then?'

'Dona Branca said I can't have a party,' Pequena answered, disappointed.

Seu Mineiro poured a ladle of small bits of papaya, banana, apples and melon into a plastic cup, filling half of it. 'Why not? It is your birthday!' He filled the rest of the cup with blackberry milk, offering the first cup to Carmem.

'She doesn't want people to know my age.' Pequena kept her eyes to the ground.

'Only because Sergeant Armando told her that if you want to stay here, we have to keep quiet about how old you are,' Zulmira explained.

'I don't mind not having a party! Zulmira said she is going to make me a cake! A chocolate one.'

'A chocolate cake?' Seu Mineiro looked at Zulmira. 'Can you make chocolate cake, Zulmira?' He closed the lid of his trolley and leaned against the porch.

'Zulmira can make all types of cake. She can even make icing for it!' Pequena said.

The following morning, the girls were all on the porch. Branquinha and Pequena sat on the banister waiting for Seu Mineiro while Jandaia painted Carmem's nails.

'Maybe he's sold out and he's not coming down here today.' Pequena didn't like waiting. 'What if he hasn't got apples left?'

'Don't be silly, Pequena. Seu Mineiro would never sell out before coming to see Carmem. He will have your apple. The only place he goes before coming here is to the Hotel das Aguias where he unloads most of his stock. He is just late.'

'I hope his wheelbarrow hasn't lost its front wheel again,' Carmem said, looking to see if Seu Mineiro was coming up the road. 'Last time it happened, he was stuck with his fruit and veggies and the wheelbarrow in the street.'

'There he is! There he is!' Pequena ran up the road to meet the streetseller. 'Seu Mineiro,' the entire village could hear Pequena calling for the grocery man, 'have you got any apples left?'

'Ah Pequena, no apple today. The plane didn't bring any.' Seu Mineiro stopped the wheelbarrow outside the porch.

'No apple today?' Pequena's mouth dropped open, her eyes disappointed.

'Instead,' Seu Mineiro wiped his forehead with a white handkerchief, 'they sent me a weird fruit. Let me see if I can find it.' His hands reached into the fabric sack hanging on the handle of the wheelbarrow.

Pequena's face lit up. 'What have you got in that bag, Seu Mineiro?'

The tall man looked at Pequena, his lips hiding a smile, his black hand holding something inside the bag, teasing the young girl. 'Happy birthday!' Seu Mineiro said, offering Pequena a pear.

'A pear!' Pequena screamed. 'My favourite fruit!'

Carmem smiled. 'Pequena, are you not going to say "thank you"?'

'Zulmira, look what Seu Mineiro gave me!' Pequena was too busy running to the kitchen to thank the generous grocery man.

Indian Rosa

Branquinha was sitting in the kitchen writing a letter while Pequena practised her handwriting when they heard the screams. They couldn't quite figure out what the woman was shouting about.

'... going to kill him!' The voice screamed clearer this time.

'Oh God. She's back!' Zulmira stood up, running out of the kitchen, followed by Branquinha, Carmem and Pequena.

'Who's back?' Branquinha asked Carmem.

'It's Indian Rosa,' Carmem explained. 'We were all hoping she'd settle down when she moved to the mines with Matias, João Preto's brother.'

'She's crazy,' Pequena whispered.

'She's not crazy, Pequena,' Carmem interrupted. 'She's just... uhm, a bit... different!'

'She's always saying she is going to kill someone! Dona Branca said...' Pequena was interrupted by a loud bang followed by screams.

When they got to the salon, a small woman was kneeling on the floor, trying to hold a man who was bleeding, a knife still stuck in his back.

'You see what you've done now, you crazy woman!' Murilo shouted. 'Matias, don't move or you'll push the knife further into your back.'

'Carmem, get me some sheets and towels!' Zulmira started shouting orders. 'Pequena go and get Dr Hans.'

'Does anyone know where Dona Branca is?' someone asked.

'Oh my god, what have I done to him?' Indian Rosa screamed, trying to hold Matias, her long black hair soaking in the pool of blood. 'Oh God, don't let him die.'

'Someone get this mad woman from here before I kill her myself!' Murilo shouted holding Matias and pressing a kitchen towel harder on one of his wounds.

'For God's sake, Murilo, take the knife out!' Matias begged.

'No, Matias. We must leave it there until the doctor comes,' Zulmira tried to comfort Matias.

'Please take the knife out,' the bleeding man moaned loudly.

'I will take it out, love... please forgove me.' India Rosa was crying.

'You are going to end up killing him for sure, you idiotic neurotic bitch.' Murilo pushed the small woman aside.

'Matias, the knife is at least five centimetres in and if we take it out you might bleed to death.' Zulmira held Matias's hand.

'Let's turn him to his side so he can't move backwards and push the knife further in,' Murilo suggested.

'Very slowly so the knife doesn't go further in...' Murilo didn't look strong enough to hold Matias.

Once they moved the injured man to a safer position, Zulmira unbuttoned his shirt so they could see the wounds but all they saw was blood flowing from the cuts.

'I think I'm going to die...' Matias's voice was growing weaker.

'Don't move, love, don't move.' Zulmira stroked Matias's hair. 'Just rest.' She didn't let go of his hand.

Seu Geraldo, the dark and short pharmacist who lived across the road, arrived and, after a brief examination of Matias' wounds, said, 'I need to give him an injection to stop the bleeding before we take the knife out.'

'We called for Dr Hans,' Murilo told him.

'Dr Hans won't treat him.' Seu Geraldo cut Matias's shirt with a pair of scissors.

'What do you mean, he won't treat him?' Murilo challenged Seu Geraldo. 'He's João Preto's brother They have the money to pay.'

Seu Geraldo didn't reply. Instead he opened his bag and told Zulmira, 'He needs an injection to stop the bleeding...'

'You're not giving him anything!' Murilo shut Seu Geraldo's bag. 'A real doctor is on his way.'

Seu Geraldo, still bending over Matias, looked up and, carefully choosing his words, said, 'Son, Dr Hans won't treat Matias because he's a black man.'

'Doctors are not like that,' Murilo replied. 'He'll treat Matias.'

'We'll need some towels and boiled water.' Seu Geraldo paid no attention to Murilo.

Carmem put the towels on the chair next to Seu Geraldo. 'I'll get some boiling water,' she said, heading to the kitchen.

'Young woman,' Seu Geraldo spoke to Branquinha, 'go and find a couple of pillows.'

'The doctor is here.' Pequena came running through the door.

'A negro!' Everyone turned around to look at the tall, fat blond man standing at the door. 'You call me here to treat a negro?' His wide face was red. 'If you think I am going to dirty my hands and touch him, think again.' He turned round and walked away.

'You're not leaving this place without treating him.' Indian Rosa had taken Dona Branca's shotgun from behind the bar and was pointing it straight at the doctor. 'And if he dies, you die too.'

Nobody tried to stop Indian Rosa.

'Seu Geraldo, supervise him.' Indian Rosa looked so calm and controlled.

Without saying anything, Seu Geraldo opened his case again and took out a syringe, quickly filling it, and passed it to the doctor.

'You do it, yourself,' the doctor told Seu Geraldo.

'This will help stop the bleeding, Matias.' Seu Geraldo gave Matias the injection.

It took over an hour for the doctor and Seu Geraldo to finish treating Matias. 'I want my money now,' Doctor Hans said to Murilo.

'You'll get your money once he's better.' Indian Rosa pointed the shotgun at him again.

'I can't guarantee he won't die. If he gets an infection there is nothing I can do about it.' The doctor left, his face redder than when he first arrived.

'I'll come back in a couple of hours to check up on you,' Seu Geraldo said to Matias. 'Try to rest now.'

When João Preto arrived and found out what Indian Rosa had done to his brother, he said, 'Matias has to face the consequences of his own actions. If he wants to sleep with other women he should not have got together with a woman like Indian Rosa.'

At dinner time, Branca told João Preto how Dr Hans had treated his brother. João Preto went quiet for a minute or so and when he answered, he had the calmest of the voices.

'Branca, we black people learn to live with such insults very early in life. What really matters is that Matias is now on his way to recovery.'

For days, Indian Rosa nursed Matias. She bathed and fed him like a baby until he was well enough to go back to camp.

When he left, he took Indian Rosa with him and everyone was relieved. They worried that she would stay behind to kill Dr Hans.

'For some people, death isn't enough,' João Preto said to Indian Rosa before she left. 'His punishment will come sooner than you think.'

Pequena Cinderella

'Branquinha, Branquinha, wake up. Pequena's eating glass again.' It was the third time that month that Murilo had to call Branquinha to stop Pequena biting into raw glass. Branquinha's overnight client had already left, so she jumped out of bed and followed Murilo.

Branquinha could hear Pequena's painful sobs from outside her room. She sounded like a hurt animal. Carmem stood in the corridor, by Pequena's bedroom door. 'She won't listen to me!'

Branquinha knocked on the door. 'Pequena, it's me, Branquinha. Can I come in?' Branquinha's voice was no more than a whisper.

There was no reply, but a few seconds later Branquinha and Murilo heard the key turning in the lock.

Branquinha listened to Pequena's heavy breathing and her teeth biting into the glass. She turned the door knob, pushed the door open and as she went inside, the candle in her hand lit up the room.

'Oh, my Pequena.' Branquinha removed the broken beer glass from the young girl's hand, taking care not to cut Pequena's lips, and placed it in the chamber pot next to the bed, as quietly as possible. Unrolling some toilet paper from the bedside table, she took a large piece and started picking the small pieces of chewed glass from Pequena's mouth.

Branquinha gently wiped the blood and saliva from Pequena's chin. 'Let me take the glass out of your mouth,' Branquinha whispered while she stroked Pequena's hair.

Pequena sat up and as she spat blooded pieces of glass into the white enamelled chamber pot, Branquinha brought the candle closer to Pequena's face near the mouth, hoping that the girl had not swallowed any. She picked each piece of glass, bit by bit, and carefully removed some pieces that were sticking into Pequena's tongue. Branquinha could still see the marks from the last time Pequena had bitten into a glass and cut her tongue so badly that she couldn't speak for days.

'Here is some sugary water.' Carmem came into the room offering a glass of water.

'No, Carmem, she must not drink now. If there is any glass in her mouth she'll swallow it when she drinks the sugary water. We have to wait until she calms down and agrees to rinse her mouth first,' Branquinha whispered to Carmem. Pequena was still sobbing.

'Keep the noise down. If Cloé hears her she'll go straight to Dona Branca.' Murilo came back into the room, shutting the door behind him. 'You are stupid, Pequena! If you want to die, jump into the river, but don't try to eat glass!'

'Murilo! Now is not the time.' Branquinha wrapped her arms around Pequena.

'She's crazy, this one. Last week, it was because one of her customers hit her, today is because Martinho didn't come last night. If Dona Branca finds out she's doing it again she'll throw her out and she'll have to go back to her father's house.'

'Please don't... I don't want to go back to my father's house. I don't want to get pregnant by my own father.' Pequena sobbed louder as she buried her head into Branquinha's shoulders.

'What's going on over there?' They heard Cloé's voice from across the corridor.

Murilo and Carmem quickly left the room while Branquinha placed a pillow on the corner of the bed and lay down with Pequena.

'Carmem's client has been sick.' Branquinha heard Murilo explaining to Cloé. Branquinha and Pequena kept quiet as they listened to Carmem's door closing and Murilo's footsteps along the corridor.

'Sing me that song your mother taught you, Branquinha. The one with the ring of roses, the clown and the sad girl.'

'I can't sing now because if Cloé is still awake she'll hear us. Let's rinse your mouth and spit all the water out. I'll tell you Cinderella's story again, OK?'

Branquinha lifted the glass of water to Pequena's mouth and brought the chamber pot nearer.

Pequena's face showed the pain that the broken glass had caused in her mouth. She didn't complain, though, and after a few more rinses, Branquinha examined her mouth, looking for any more pieces of glass.

'Now you can drink the sugary water that Carmem brought.'

'You will tell me the story then?'

'Yes. I will. Let's lie down now. If you close your eyes like last time, you'll see the dress even better.'

Pequena closed her eyes and she could see Pequena Cinderella talking to the birds and squirrels in the forest while she was surrounded by the butterflies flying around near the stream.

'Once upon a time there was a beautiful girl called Soraia but everyone called her Pequena Cinderella. Her mother died when she was young."

As Branquinha continued with her story she could hear the water of the river running under the room. It was a soothing sound and she hoped Pequena would fall asleep soon. Her own eyes were tired.

'It was the very last house and Prince Martinho's last hope of finding his beloved Cinderella. He tried out the shoe on the two step-sisters and when it didn't fit, he was so sad. He walked out of the house with no hopes left. As he mounted his horse, he heard a beautiful voice coming from the orchards.'

'Was she singing *Children's Garden*?' Pequena interrupted in a tired voice.

'No, she was not. She was singing the pumpkin song. She was looking after her mother's kitchen garden and she always sang the pumpkin song when she tended the pumpkin plant. She sang in her pretty voice and when the Prince heard her, he knew straight away he had found Pequena Cinderella. He ran to the kitchen garden and found her there, tending to the pumpkins. He hugged her close and, taking his cape off, he covered her.'

'You forgot the bit where Martinho put the shoe on my foot,' Pequena reminded her, almost asleep.

By the time Branquinha finished the story, Pequena was fast asleep. Branquinha moved her legs out of the bed trying not to wake

Pequena up. She pulled the sheets over Pequena's shoulders, blew the candle out and left the room.

Princess Diana

Murilo, Pequena and Branquinha sat on the porch watching the men carry furniture into The Palace, the brothel across the road. The owner of The Palace had recently painted its façade a golden yellow, the doors and windows in a bright red and there had been a lot of refurbishment inside.

Branca and Murilo were worried that a more luxurious establishment would attract the richer gold miners and Casa da Branca would miss out on the best clients.

'They have a new girl in The Palace!' Carmem told them when she arrived from the ice cream shop. 'One of their girls went to buy ice cream and I heard her saying a new woman has just arrived with a lot of furniture.'

'She has a black and gold bed and a red velvet sofa!' Pequena said in surprise. 'She must be rich.'

'Don't be silly, Pequena! There is no such a thing as a rich whore.' Murilo dragged his chair to get a better view of The Palace.

'Dona Branca's rich,' Carmem said.

'Dona Branca is not a whore!' Murilo and Pequena replied almost at the same time.

'She charges João Preto,' Carmem argued.

'She does not charge him! He gives her gifts.' Murilo rolled his eyes. 'Dona Branca is not a whore.'

'Quiet,' Branquinha whispered. 'If she finds out you're calling her a whore, you'll be in big trouble.'

'I didn't call her a whore,' Murilo replied.

'Who's not a whore?' They heard Cloé's voice coming from inside the salon.

Murilo stood up and leant against the beam supporting the porch's roof.

'We're talking about the rich whore who is moving in to The Palace,' Branquinha answered. 'Come and see. She has some pretty amazing furniture.'

'She's so rich that she even has a lampshade!' Pequena told Cloé.

At dinner time, everyone was talking about the new girl in the Palace. Dona Branca wanted to know where she came from and asked Murilo to find out more about her.

'Baronesa brought her all the way from Curitiba and she's only agreed to move to The Palace after Baronesa told her that the girls at The Palace all have titles in their names. She's going to be "Princess Diana".' Murilo paused and added some cassava flour to the juices of the fish casserole on his plate. 'She had a tantrum when Baronesa wanted to put her in the Queen's Suite.'

'But isn't the Queen's suite the biggest one?' Dona Branca asked.

Everyone looked at Murilo waiting for him to finish chewing his food.

'The stupid girl thought a princess was more important than a queen,' Murilo finally said laughing.

'A princess is very important!' Pequena interrupted.

'Queens are mothers of princesses and that is why they are more important,' Branquinha explained to Pequena.

'Ah!' Pequena smiled and started picking the bones out of her fish.

'I told you she was rich,' Carmem said. 'With a name like that she will be very busy.'

In the evening when Dona Branca arrived in the salon she asked Murilo if he had heard any more news about Princess Diana.

'Baronesa had to change the name of the suite to "Princess Diana Wing".' Murilo repeated what he had heard from Serginho who did the hair of one of the girls in The Palace.

'This is not good for us, Murilo. When word gets out that The Palace has a girl called Princess Diana, we'll lose business. After all, Princess Diana is such an icon.'

And she was right, for night after night they saw The Palace packed with men, while her place was only visited by the most loyal customers or the poorer clients who could not afford the fees charged by The Palace.

She was even more worried when The Palace closed for three days for even more refurbishment.

'They put toilets in three bedrooms only last month and they are going to refurbish again?' Dona Branca asked.

One of Cloé's clients told them Baronesa said that The Palace was going to change its name to The Golden Palace and everything was going to be gold.

On the re-opening night, Dona Branca threw a party with free food and although a few customers turned up, they left for The Palace immediately after eating.

For most of the night the girls sat in the empty room and even when Carmem sang there were very few customers. Now and again one of the girls would walk to the front door and watch The Palace through the curtains.

When Murilo closed for the night and took the money to Dona Branca he sounded concerned. 'Things aren't good at all, Dona Branca. Tonight Carmem saw two of Cloé's customers in The Palace.'

'Murilo, I've been in business long enough to know that the novelty will soon wear off.' Dona Branca was remarkably relaxed. She counted the money, scribbled her signature in Murilo's books and put the money in the safe on the wall behind her bedside cabinet.

'Let's give ourselves a bit of time. Things will sort themselves out,' she said to Murilo before bidding him goodnight.

Murilo walked away from Dona Branca's room thinking, for the first time, Dona Branca was wrong.

Nobody knew where the rumours started but when the gold miners heard that The Palace was jinxed they stopped going in. Word went round that any miner who adventured in the place wouldn't find any gold in their mines. Soon the miners stopped going to The Palace and, with the exception of a few miners from other areas who didn't know about the curse, the place was empty.

The end came when Pequena ran into the room shouting, 'The

police van has just arrived outside The Palace and five policemen went in, including Sergeant Armando.'

Everyone went out to the porch to find out what was happening.

'The police are after a robber from the south,' a passer-by said.

Murilo saw Zulmira coming down the road with a bag of shopping. She stopped outside The Palace and talked to one of the policemen.

'It's Princess Diana. We found out that she's a thief. All the furniture she has was stolen from her previous boss's house.

'So she's not rich at after all,' Pequena said loudly.

They heard her screams before they saw her.

'You are hurting me!' Princess Diana came out of The Palace with her hands cuffed behind her back, her short blonde hair in a complete mess. 'Go back inside your filthy holes, you bunch of ugly whores!' she shouted to Branquinha and the others who stood across the street.

Murilo laughed. He turned to Carmem and Branquinha and said, 'I told you, there is no such a thing as a rich whore!'

The New Cook

Branquinha was sitting at the kitchen table helping Fafá, the blonde and big-bosomed temporary cook, to prepare lunch.

'Zulmira had better come back from her holiday or I'll die of starvation.' Murilo was convinced that Fafá was cooking bacon with the beans, and he had asked Branquinha to spy on the new cook. He didn't eat pork and he didn't trust anyone other than Zulmira to cook for him.

Dona Branca was lucky to find a cook at such short notice because there were only a handful of women in Jardim do Ouro who were prepared to work hard and not give in to the temptation of having an "easy life".

Branquinha listened to Fafá's unstoppable banter while she chopped the onions.

'I liked working at the Hotel das Aguias but Dona Loura, the owner's wife, found out he was cheating on her and it was only a matter of time that someone would tell her who he was cheating with.'

'Did everyone know about it then?' Branquinha asked Fafá.

'You know how these things happen: somebody finds out and all of a sudden everybody knows. We tried to hide it, but the chambermaids saw us coming out of a room together a few times. He told them that he was helping me to move some of the furniture around, but they are not stupid. How often do you actually move the beds in a hotel?' Fafá giggled.

Murilo, appearing from nowhere, put his head into the room and said, 'If I were you, I would be worried. I heard Dona Loura is fearsome. She once beat a guy so badly he had to be taken to

101

hospital; all because he opened her hen pen and she lost a hen and some chickens.'

Fafá went quiet for a while and, once she'd put the beans in the pressure cooker, Branquinha left. Murilo's beans would be safe for an hour or so. She would be back before lunch to keep an eye on Fafá when she would season the beans just before serving.

They were all eating dinner when they heard the loud voices. Murilo jumped out of his chair so fast that it fell back on the floor. He disappeared up the corridor followed by Branquinha, Fafá and Carmem.

'Dona Branca, let me through or I won't be responsible for what I do next! I know she's working here. I know she's in there and I want to kill that whore.' There was no doubt that, whoever the woman was, she was very angry.

It wasn't until Fafá started running towards the back of the house that Murilo, Carmem and Branquinha realised the angry woman was after Fafá.

Dona Branca had placed herself in the door between the salon and the corridor that led through the rest of the house and wasn't going to let the woman, Dona Loura, in. 'This is my house and I am in charge.' Dona Branca's hand held firmly on to the doorframe.

'Let me in, or I'll kill you too!' Dona Loura waved a knife up in the air.

'Here I'm the boss. If I say you're not coming in, you won't come in. Not while I have blood running through my veins!' Dona Branca's voice sounded more confident now that she had Murilo and the girls all behind her forming a barrier.

'To kill Dona Branca you'll have to go over my dead body.' Murilo went past under Dona Branca's arm and stood in front of her.

'I want that whore. I gave her a job and she tried to steal my husband from me. Let me through!'

'I said no and I meant no!' Dona Branca insisted. 'If you are going to kill every woman your husband sleeps with, the village will soon be half empty. Go back home.'

Someone had gone to call Dona Loura's husband and after a few minutes he arrived and took her home with him. She screamed all the way home, complaining that he had brought shame to their home and embarrassed their family.

Fafá didn't come out from under Branquinha's bed where she had hidden until Dona Branca came to tell her Dona Loura had gone.

Fafá was worried for a few days and refused to go out in the street and didn't want to do the shopping, which was one of her jobs as a cook. After a week, she gathered enough courage to venture to the butcher's on the condition Branquinha went with her. They took over twenty minutes for a trip that should take five; all because they had to avoid Dona Loura's hotel and go via the back of the houses.

On the second week, when Fafá and Branquinha were coming back from their daily shopping, they spotted Dona Loura. She didn't see them at first and continued to walk down the street. Fafá and Branquinha quickly left the street and entered the first door they found.

It was a large garage with several cars with open bonnets waiting to be fixed. Branquinha called out but the loud music coming from the radio masked her voice and nobody came to help. She looked around the walls, trying to spot a door on the walls covered in posters of naked women.

Fafá was shaking and as Branquinha pulled her hand and dragged her to hide behind one of the many cars, they saw Dona Loura standing at the front door with her blonde hair in total disarray, her face red as if her blood was boiling underneath the skin.

She shouted out something but Branquinha couldn't make out what she said. Dona Loura's angry eyes scanned the room, finally resting on the car which Fafá and Branquinha were hiding behind. Dona Loura moved forward, heading towards them and Fafá, looking from under the cars, realised that Dona Loura was very near indeed.

She got up and ran, trying to make it to the door. Dona Loura saw her and, grabbing a bucket of engine oil, threw it on Fafá, reaching her before she got to the door. Fafá slipped on the oil and fell on her back. She lay there, still, covered in engine oil, from head to toe.

When Dona Loura put her hand into her bag, Branquinha

breathed in and froze. She imagined Dona Loura was reaching for a knife or another weapon to kill Fafá.

'Please Dona Loura, don't kill her. You'll have blood on your hands for the rest of your life,' Branquinha implored. 'She's not worth it.'

'You are right.' Dona Loura walked close and bent over Fafá's face covered in black engine oil. 'I'm not going to kill this whore. You ruined my marriage, but you won't ruin my life.' Dona Loura picked up a cauliflower from the bag, stuck the stalk into Fafá's mouth and walked away.

The radio stopped and Branquinha heard a man's voice shouting, 'What is going on here?'

The Visitors

Branquinha was sitting at the kitchen table picking the beans while Pequena worked on her sums.

'I can't wait for Zulmira to come back. I really miss her cooking,' Pequena said before she remembered Branquinha was in charge of the kitchen since Fafá ran away from the village. 'No offence, Branquinha. I like your cooking, but Zulmira's is better.'

'I know.' Branquinha poured the beans into the empty bowl and covered it with water. 'I miss her food too.'

'Why do you soak the beans? Zulmira doesn't do that,' Pequena questioned Branquinha.

'Because they'll cook quicker tomorrow and we'll save a lot of gas.'

'My mum used to do that. I never knew why.'

'Your mum's a thrifty cook, Pequena. Now stop talking and get on with the sums while I knead the bread.'

'Are you going to put bacon in the bread again?' Pequena asked Branquinha.

'No way! Not after Murilo threw a fit like he did the other day, even though I made a whole loaf without bacon for him.'

'I like it with the bits of bacon, though,' the younger girl complained.

'If I don't put bacon in, you can enjoy it with pumpkin jam instead.' Branquinha reached for a large pumpkin from the cupboard. 'Look what Seu Mineiro brought us this morning.'

'Oh Branquinha, please teach me how to make pumpkin jam with coconut. I love it, and Martinho loves it, too.' Pequena pushed her notebook away. 'I want to learn so I can cook for him when we get married.'

'I'll teach you after you finish your sums today.'

'Please, Branquinha, I want to learn it now. It'll take me ages to finish my sums.'

'You're good with numbers, Pequena.' Branquinha placed the notebook back in front of Pequena. 'It won't take...'

'Branquinha, quick, quick, come outside!' Carmem stuck her head around the door before running towards the front of the house with Branquinha and Pequena following in her footsteps.

'What's going on?' Murilo came out of his room, buttoning his jeans.

'The Federal Police are here, with three cars and they brought some strange men with them. They are speaking foreign and one of them is wearing a kind of fabric plate on his head,' Ana told them.

From the porch they saw three large police cars parked in the middle of the road, one of them directly under Seu Fernando's new red awning.

'Oh, my god. What's the Federal Police doing here?' Jandaia joined them on the porch.

'Why is that man wearing that stupid thing on his head?' Pequena asked Branquinha.

'The stupid thing is called a kippa and those men are Jews.' Murilo didn't wait for Branquinha's reply.

'Jews?' Pequena twisted her face. 'What are they doing here? Don't they live where Jesus was born?'

'That is a good question. What are they doing here?' Murilo asked.

It didn't take long for them to find out why the Federal Police were there. Half an hour later they saw Dr Hans, the racist doctor, being dragged down the road, handcuffed and pushed into the back seat of one of the police cars.

'He's a Nazi,' one of the policemen told them. 'The Jews have been chasing him for a long time for his war crimes.'

'Those Jews are Nazi hunters and they find the holocaust perpetrators and bring the Federal Police with them so they can be arrested and extradited back to Europe to be prosecuted for their crimes,' Murilo explained.

'How do you know all this stuff?' Branquinha asked Murilo.

Murilo didn't reply. Instead he went back inside.

'Murilo is clever, Branquinha. He knows everything.' Pequena climbed on the banister.

For the rest of the day nobody talked about anything else other than Dr Hans' arrest. Everyone was surprised that he was a war criminal and everybody was wondering how the police had managed to find him in such a remote place.

'Sooner or later people like Dr Hans get what they deserve,' Dona Branca said with a smile. 'Let's celebrate! Murilo, a round of drinks for everyone, on the house!'

Murilo poured drinks for everyone but he could not stop wondering how did the Jews come to find out that Dr Hans was living in Jardim do Ouro.

It wasn't until a few days later when João Preto came to settle the drinks bill that Murilo realised who was responsible for Dr Hans' arrest.

The Church

Branquinha looked at the church down the road with its blue wooden walls and white windows matching the picket fence at the front, the clean plot around the building showing how much the members of the congregation cared about their church.

She stood by the small blue gate, gathering enough courage to go inside.

It was near Christmas and Branquinha had been living in Jardim do Ouro for six months. She missed going to church and on that Saturday she had got up very early to travel to Moraes de Almeida to get to church in time for the service. The roads were very muddy and it took almost two hours for the car to get there.

Her conservative Protestant upbringing didn't let her forget that she needed to be aware of her sins if she wanted to find peace within herself. She longed for the peaceful atmosphere, for the beautiful hymns and the comforting words of the sermons promising a better future for everyone who followed God. But above all, Branquinha wanted forgiveness for the life she led.

There was music coming from a black tape player in the corner and Branquinha recognized the songs of a popular evangelical singing group. She sat on the last bench at the back of the church, pulling the hem of her skirt down, hoping her dress was modest enough and she didn't give away the fact that she was a woman of easy virtue. She wrapped Zulmira's shawl round her shoulders, trying to ensure nobody noticed the sleeveless dress.

A tall and thin man stood up and turned off the music. 'My brothers, let us all sing!'

The hymn chosen was one of her mother's favourites and

Branquinha knew the words by heart. She stood up and together with everyone else she sang about having Jesus in her heart wherever she went.

A young woman with two little children and a baby arrived and sat next to Branquinha. They smiled at each other. The mother reminded her of her friend Sara who always sat at the back with her children not to disturb the service when the baby cried or her young daughter needed the toilet.

The service continued with a short woman, dressed in a white floral skirt below the knee which made her look even shorter, coming to the front and reading a piece about how the church needed to raise money to build an orphanage in Africa. Then an elderly man came round with a basket collecting alms for the construction of the orphanage. Branquinha put a large folded note in and the old man nodded his head and smiled at her.

After half an hour or so, Branquinha started to relax. *These are all good people*, she said to herself. The familiar reading and songs made her feel calm and almost forgiven. *God will understand.* The service proceeded while a couple of mothers tried to control their children and an older lady whispered to another.

The tall and thin man stood up again. 'Now brothers and sisters, I give you our dear Brother Paulo who is visiting us all the way from Curitiba'.

Brother Paulo, an unusually tall and large man, took the pulpit. His grey hair lent him an air of wisdom and his deep voice made everyone pay immediate attention.

'Brothers and sisters, in a few days it will be Christmas and as we celebrate the birth of our Lord Jesus Christ, we should remind ourselves of his teachings and our need for tolerance and love to others if we want to join Him in Paradise.'

The sermon was beautiful and Brother Paulo had everyone clinging to each and every word of his and, by the end of it, Branquinha felt glad she had come to the church.

'Now, brothers and sisters, let's close our eyes and pray that God forgive us for our sins and help us to become better people.'

Branquinha knelt on the hard cement floor and prayed, *'Please God, please God, help me be as good as these people and learn with* them so I can join you and Jesus in Paradise. Help me make enough money to get out of this life of sin and rot that I've found myself in. Help my mother to recover her health. Help Vilson wherever he is and protect me so I can be strong and fight against the odds of my life.'

'Amen.' Brother Paulo finished his sermon.

The tall and thin man stood up again and asked the congregation: 'Any announcements?'

'I have!' The short woman with the floral white skirt who had asked for money for the orphans of Africa jumped up from her seat and, almost running, she climbed the two steps to the pulpit. 'Brothers and sisters, I'm sad to tell you all that we have let our house of God be soiled by the presence of a harlot amongst us.'

Branquinha continued seated, hoping the woman was not talking about her.

'That woman,' the large lady pointed her finger in Branquinha's direction, 'is a whore of the worst kind, my brothers and sisters.'

Branquinha was paralysed.

'She lives with the devil in a brothel in Jardim do Ouro together with Satan's daughters and her sisters in sin.'

The young mother sitting next to Branquinha grabbed hold of her child and quickly moved away.

'That woman, my brothers and sisters, is damned to hell and it is our job to ensure that she and the likes of her do not come into the sanctity of the house of our Lord.' The woman climbed down from the stage and started walking towards Branquinha, her red chin buried in her neck.

Branquinha stood up.

'Out of here, harlot, daughter of Satan! Out of here!'

That was the last time Branquinha went to a Protestant church and for a long time she could still hear the voice of the angry woman and others who joined her: *'Out of here, harlot. Out of the house of our Lord!'*

Christmas Eve and the Snake

It was the morning of Christmas Eve and everyone was in a party mood. Most of the girls had new outfits to wear and Jandaia and Carmem had booked everyone in to have a manicure and pedicure.

Zulmira, Branquinha and Pequena were in the kitchen preparing the food for Christmas supper. Everything needed to be ready for eight o'clock so they could party before the meal at midnight.

Zulmira lifted the kitchen towel covering the large baking tray and examined the leg of pork she had left marinating from the previous night. The smell of garlic, black pepper and vinegar impregnated the air.

'Pequena, could you take this tray to the salon, please?' Zulmira asked.

'I thought you said you were going to cook the pork in the oven and not at the barbecue,' Pequena said.

'I am, but I need to cook the dessert now and if I leave this meat in the kitchen, the smell of garlic will get into the crème caramel and ruin it,' Zulmira explained.

Pequena reached for the aluminium tray. 'This is heavy!'

'There's a lot of us eating today.' Zulmira drained the water from the large pan of unpeeled cooked potatoes. 'Hurry up now, I need you to come and peel these potatoes for the salad.'

The rain had stopped by the afternoon, and the sun came out so everybody was feeling the heat.

'I need another shower.' Pequena wiped her face with the wet towel wrapped around her neck.

'Showers will cool you for five minutes and then you'll be hot again,' Branquinha said to Pequena. 'You still need to wrap your Secret Santa gift for Dona Branca. Let me go and get the paper for you.'

'Do you really think she'll like the dragon lampshade?' Pequena asked Branquinha when she got back.

'Of course she will. Dona Branca loves all things with dragons on them.' Branquinha cut the sticky tape for Pequena. 'Her dressing gown has a dragon in it and so do her curtains and bedspread. So she'll love a dragon lampshade to match.'

'You'd better hurry up and get yourselves sorted before the dragon herself comes for you!' Murilo shouted from the bar hatch, tapping on his watch.

As evening arrived, a large empty drum, cut in half lengthways, was filled with the dry wood that João Preto brought with him. They set it up in the street by the porch.

'Don't use kerosene or the meat will taste foul,' João Preto said to his worker, Sorocaba. 'Go inside and ask Zulmira for some ethanol.'

A few minutes later, the firewood was burning and the orange flames leaping up the sides of the drum, crackling.

'A snake!' Carmem shouted, pointing to a red, yellow and black striped snake coming from the inside of the drum. 'Over there!' The men were quick to get their knives out of their pockets and started grabbing sticks to chase the small snake. But the snake was too fast and soon it manoeuvred its way away from the men and disappeared between the gaps in the floor.

'It must have been in the pile of wood,' João Preto said. 'Lucky it didn't bite anyone. That was a true coral snake. Its venom is lethal.'

That night, everyone was happy. The girls felt beautiful in their new dresses and shoes, and appreciated by the customers, who were drunk with fizzy cider and sweet red wine.

João Preto and Sorocaba barbequed large cuts of beef on skewers over the open fire outside the porch and, when dinner was finally served, everyone helped themselves to the generous helpings of food from the buffet that Zulmira served in the salon, while the tables were full of plates, glasses and the red napkins that Branca had bought specially for the occasion. Now and again, one would hear comments about what a great cook Zulmira was.

Just before midnight, Dona Branca stopped the country music and asked Murilo to play *Noite Feliz*[1] on the stereo. Some of them didn't know the lyrics, but they still hummed along with Carmem leading the singing.

'Only in Jardim do Ouro would you find a room full of prostitutes singing hymns and celebrating the birth of the boy Jesus,' Murilo whispered to Branquinha, laughing.

'Don't be so cynical,' Branquinha replied.

As the clock struck twelve, everyone hugged and shouted, *'Feliz Natal'* to each other. In that happy moment they forgot the families they missed, the arguments they had among themselves and all the tragedies they had been through.

Amidst all the noise, nobody heard Carmem shouting, 'The snake is back.'

It wasn't until she shouted again that people near her stood back, but Sorocaba, who had drunk more than his fair share of alcohol, carried on dancing and stepped on the snake and by the time he realised what was happening it was too late.

'Sorocaba has been bitten by the coral snake!' Carmem shouted, and this time people heard her.

Murilo turned the stereo off and someone, turning a chair upside down, managed to hit the snake and the second and third blow killed it.

They carried Sorocaba to Seu Geraldo's Pharmacy but it was too late. By the time they arrived, Sorocaba was dead.

---

1 Silent Night

The Kitchen Garden

Branquinha and Pequena were sitting in the salon watching Jandaia painting Carmem's toe nails. She had not taken her sunglasses off.

'Jandaia, where did you learn to do such a good pedicure?' Pequena asked.

'My sister is a beautician and she taught me a thing or two. One day I'll have enough money to open my own salon and leave this life.' Jandaia started coating Carmem's toenails with a layer of crimson nail polish.

'Can you dye hair?' Branquinha asked.

'Yes, I can. Why?' Jandaia turned her face away from Carmem's toes and looked at Branquinha. 'Surely you don't want to dye your hair!'

'Oh, it's not for me.' Branquinha pushed her dark brown hair behind her right ear. 'I was thinking about Dona Branca because I bleached her roots last month but I don't think she was very happy with the way I did the work. Maybe you should offer to do her hair next time.'

'Ana will soon need to have her roots done, too,' Pequena said. 'She is getting old.'

'Ana isn't old at all, Pequena,' Carmem argued.

'She is!' Pequena insisted. 'She has a lot of grey hair downstairs.'

Carmem, Branquinha and Jandaia were still laughing when Ana walked into the room.

'You'll never guess who is in the kitchen with Zulmira!'

After a few guesses the girls gave up.

'Gigi! Apparently, Davi went back to his wife and since then she's

114

been living in the shed on her allotment.'

'She was stupid to go in the first place,' Ana said. 'We all know men never leave their wives for a mistress.'

'Is she coming back?' Branquinha asked Ana.

'I don't know.' Ana raised her shoulders. 'She brought a basket full of okra, courgettes and cucumber from her kitchen garden.'

'I hate okra. I hope Zulmira doesn't make me eat it.' Pequena twisted her face in disgust. 'Come on, Branquinha, let's go to the kitchen to see if Gigi is coming back to live with us.'

Gigi was sitting at the kitchen table. She had been crying and Zulmira was holding her hand.

'Hello, Gigi,' Pequena greeted the other woman. 'Is it true that Davi left you and you are living in your shed?'

'Pequena...!'

'Don't worry, Zulmira.' Gigi blew her nose on a white handkerchief. 'Sooner or later people will find out.'

'What are you going to do?' Pequena asked.

'I don't know. I asked Dona Branca if I could come back but she said there is no room because the two spare rooms are for João Preto's staff and they are full of his things anyway.'

'Have you asked if they have any room at The Palace?'

'They don't want me there because Davi used to go there... and he left them... to come here... because of me.' The others could make almost no sense of what Gigi was saying.

'I'll talk to Dona Branca when she gets back and you might be able to stay here for a little while. João Preto's men are not due here for a few days,' Zulmira said to Gigi.

'Don't worry, Gigi.' Pequena stroked Gigi's hair. 'Things will get better. But if you stay, can you please not bring us any more okra?'

Dona Branca came to the kitchen just in time to catch Gigi. 'Sorry, Gigi, you can stay here for a couple of days but as soon as João Preto's men arrive, you have to go.' Dona Branca poured herself a glass of water from the terracotta filter at the corner. 'If João Preto finds out I'm letting one of the girls sleep and entertain clients in his room, he won't be happy.'

'I just need a few days of work so I can get some money for the coach, then I can move to another town.' Gigi was still crying. 'Two days will be enough.'

'Uhm... you can have my room. I'm...' They all turned to Ana standing at the door. 'I'm leaving the life.'

'Oh yeah, again?' Dona Branca put her hands on her hips and challenged Ana. 'I take it you've won the lottery then?'

'Not really...' Ana started, then hesitated.

'Ana, don't be stupid. You left the life once when you found the job in the bakery in Moraes de Almeida, but remember what happened?'

'It's different this time, Dona Branca.'

'Different how, Ana?' Dona Branca banged the empty glass on the table. 'You girls don't stand a chance out there. The minute things go wrong everyone blames you.'

'I know Dona Branca but...'

'Don't give me buts.' Dona Branca pointed her finger a Ana. 'Last time you got yourself a proper job I had to pay the bakery owner when he turned up demanding the money you stole from him.'

'You know I didn't steal that money, Dona Branca.' Ana's tears were running on her face.

'I know it and you know it, but everyone blames you girls for everything bad that happens in the world.'

'I'm moving back to Goiania, Dona Branca.' Ana managed to say. 'Someone promised to help me out soon.'

'Please don't tell me you are leaving because of a man, too!' Dona Branca rolled her eyes. 'Isn't this idiot here,' Dona Branca said, pointing to Gigi, 'a living proof that men are all the same and they promise you the world, but when it comes to delivering it, they always let you down?'

Nobody said anything. They all knew Dona Branca's terrible temper and the best thing to do was to stay quiet until she calmed down.

'If that is what you want, go for it. If things go wrong, don't come running back to me, because this is it!' Dona Branca said to Ana and then turned to Gigi. 'You can stay in the spare room until Ana leaves and after that you can have her room.'

Carmem, Branquinha and Pequena went up the road to help Gigi to fetch her belongings from the shed in her allotment.

Gigi's shed, about eight hundred metres up the road, was next to Seu Mineiro's allotment. The tall forest stood behind her place.

'Bloody hell, Gigi, why do you have so much okra?' Pequena asked, looking at the okra plants which leaned against the fence all around the small allotment.

'It is easy to grow and people like it,' Gigi replied.

'This is amazing, Gigi.' Branquinha stared at the straight line of green leaves on the raised beds. 'You must have worked so hard to get it all so neat like this.'

'What are you planning to do with all this okra?' Pequena pointed at the line of tall plants.

'I'll sell some to Seu Mineiro and eat the rest,' Gigi replied while she collected a red top from a drying line which ran from the shed to a fence post. 'And this is not all okra, Pequena. I've also got aubergine and peppers planted together.'

'Still, a lot of okra.'

When they got back to the Casa da Branca, Pequena went straight to her room complaining of an upset stomach.

'Drink this.' Zulmira gave Pequena a glass of water with bubbling antacid salts in it. 'Have you been eating too much chocolate again, Pequena?'

'No,' Pequena answered sheepishly.

'If you're worried about having to eat okra, don't worry. I was planning to let you off anyway,' Zulmira said before shutting the door behind her.

Dona Branca's Son Comes to Visit

Carmem elbowed Branquinha, lifting her chin towards Murilo. He was crossing the salon towards Gigi's corner.

Gigi was not the friendly type and since coming back after Davi dumped her she had become even more difficult, preferring to keep herself to herself, so people very rarely spoke to her. Murilo bent down and whispered something in her ear.

'No!' Gigi jumped up and stared wildly at Murilo. 'When?' She sounded scared.

'This Friday.' Murilo lifted his eyebrows and pressed his lips together.

'I'm not staying here!' Gigi folded her arms and shook her head.

'Dona Branca said you can go away for a few days. She won't fine you.'

'After all that happened, that's the least she could do.' Gigi uncrossed her arms just to, immediately cross them again.

'No need to make such a fuss, Gigi. You go away for a few days and we'll let you know when he leaves.' Murilo sounded conciliatory.

'I don't want to go away.' Gigi pouted. 'I need to make enough money so I can move out of here for good.'

'He's her son, Gigi.' Murilo sighed. 'You're lucky she let you stay after what happened.'

'After what happened?' Gigi had tears in her eyes. 'It was all his fault!' Gigi stood up and stamped out of the room.

'She's gone hysterical.' Murilo twisted his lips, closing his eyes and lifting his eyebrows.

'I'm not surprised, Murilo,' Carmem replied.

'What happened?' Branquinha wanted to know.

Murilo and Carmem remained in silence.

'Ah, a secret about Dona Branca's son,' Branquinha guessed.

'You may as well tell her, Murilo,' Carmem said. 'She needs to know in case he takes a shine to her, too.'

Murilo crossed his arms so Branquinha didn't ask anything. It was obvious that the subject was sensitive.

'Murilo, tell her!' Carmem insisted.

'Guilherme, Dona Branca's son, has some bad habits...' Murilo finally gave in.

'Bad habits?' Murilo was interrupted by Carmem's indignation. 'That's a new name for gagging the poor girl, tying her to the bed, then trying to set fire to her after burning her legs with his cigarette!'

'He's nasty, we all know that, but we have to remember he's Dona Branca's son!'

'Nasty doesn't cover it, Murilo.' Carmem was not giving in. 'The man's demented!'

'Demented or not, he's still Dona Branca's son and if she's letting him come back who are you to say no?'

Carmem stood up swearing under her breath in Spanish and she walked out of the room. 'If he comes near me I'll do what Indian Rosa did and show him the knife. He almost killed Gigi last time.'

'She's right,' Murilo admitted to Branquinha. 'If it wasn't for Zulmira keeping an eye on what was happening, he'd probably have killed Gigi that night.'

Branquinha didn't say anything, but she hoped Guilherme didn't like her.

Carmem and Branquinha were in the kitchen watching Zulmira sharpening her knives when they heard Dona Branca screaming in happiness.

'Gui, my son! You look so handsome!'

He greeted his mum with a question. 'Have you got new girls in, Mother?'

'Oh Gui! You know you're not supposed to touch the girls in the house.'

The sound of their voices disappeared as Dona Branca and Guilherme moved away from the front door.

'What do we do if he takes an interest in us?'

'He won't touch me.' Carmem sounded very sure. 'He knows what Paraguayan people are like. If he dares to do anything to me, my Paraguayan friends will make mincemeat of him.'

'Gui likes kissing.' Zulmira wiped a small knife. 'If he shows any interest in you and comes anywhere near you, be ready.'

'What can I do?' Branquinha passed the peeled onions to Zulmira.

Zulmira didn't speak until she'd finished chopping the garlic with her newly sharpened knife. 'I have the perfect weapon.'

Gui slept the whole day and didn't get up until past nine the following night.

'Murilo, Gui's dinner is cold now. Go to Seu Didi's cart and bring Gui two beef skewers with manioc,' Dona Branca asked.

'Make it four.' Guilherme shouted from the chair where he was semi-lying with his feet crossed over another chair. 'One of them chicken.'

'He doesn't do chicken.'

'Damn this fucking shithole. I'll have to have four of whatever crap he sells.'

Branquinha watched Guilherme from afar, listening to him curse the village and its inhabitants. She hoped a client would walk in and she'd have the excuse to go back to her room.

'Why are you hiding in there, Branquinha?' Cloé said from across the room. 'We're short of girls tonight and we need you on the dance floor.'

Branquinha slowly walked to the room, shy, with her head bending down. As she passed Guilherme she noticed him staring at his fingers and muttering about what a dirty place it was.

'Sit next to me, Branquinha.' Cloé tapped on the chair next to her. 'You heard about our Gui then!' Cloé asked Branquinha.

Branquinha nodded.

'He is a psychopath. If a man treated me that badly I'd kill him,' Cloé said loud enough for others to hear. 'But not before I cut his bits off with a blunt knife and threw them piece by piece to the piranhas in the river.' She chuckled.

Murilo arrived with the skewers of smoking meat; bringing in the smell of the small pieces of tender beef which had marinated for hours before they were cooked in the heat of the charcoal.

Branquinha shifted her chair slightly so she could see Guilherme. She watched him biting the beef with the end of his teeth, without touching it with his lips, and carefully pulling each piece of meat away from the small wooden skewer.

'Why people have to put fucking garlic in every fucking shit they cook?' Guilherm spat his food out on the floor, the chewed piece of meat almost landing on Branquinha's foot.

Branquinha was terrified and at the same time fascinated by the man. He ate with his mouth open and Branquinha was hypnotized by the movement of his teeth grinding the meat in a steady, slow motion.

'The man's a monster,' Carmem whispered.

'How did he manage to hurt Gigi like that?'

'He tied her hands back.'

'Why did she let him do it?'

'He promised not to hurt her,' Carmem covered her mouth while she spoke. 'But once she was tied, he gagged her only to take the gag off to shove his bits down her throat.'

'What a horrible man,' Branquinha replied.

'He burnt her,' Carmem continued. 'Then he hit her with his belt until she was bleeding and squeezed her neck so badly that she had the marks for weeks.'

'My goodness!' Branquinha understood why Gigi was so keen to avoid Guilherme.

'She was so ill that she couldn't speak and walk properly for days,' Carmem said. 'We must keep away from him.'

Branquinha looked towards Guilherme again. He was standing up, staring at her. He pushed his plate away and the last kebab rolled on the floor.

As Branquinha watched him walking towards her, licking his fingers. She remembered Zulmira's advice.

'Well, well... what have we got here? A fresh flower?'

Branquinha had never seen anyone smiling that way. She shivered. Her hand reached into her pocket and she found what she was looking for.

He walked closer.

Branquinha quickly put the clove of garlic in her mouth and started to chew.

Ana Says Goodbye

'Ana's leaving on Monday.' Dona Branca came into the kitchen and told Zulmira, Murilo and Branquinha. 'We are having her leaving party on Saturday.'

'Good for her.' Zulmira took her glasses off and lifted her gaze away from the pile of beans on the table to look at Dona Branca. 'She's got the money then?'

'Yes,' Dona Branca confirmed.

'I heard Indio struck big gold in his mine.' Murilo's eyes wandered sideways. 'He was here yesterday. Maybe he gave her the rest of the money she needed to go home.'

'Come with me, Murilo.' Dona Branca walked to the door. 'We need to go shopping for the party.'

For a while Zulmira and Branquinha sat at the table picking the beans.

'It's good for Ana that she can finally go home.' Zulmira broke the silence.

'Yes but what I can't understand is why someone would give a woman so much money when he hardly knows her?'

'Branquinha, in a place like this we form strong bonds with people we hardly know.' Zulmira moved the bad beans to a separate pile.

Branquinha thought about the day when Zulmira lent her the money to send to her mother. 'Yes, like when you lent me that money to send to my mum,' Branquinha said, looking at Zulmira.

'That was nothing, child.' Zulmira got up and started washing the beans in the sink.

'I'll never forget what you did for me, Zulmira.' Branquinha stood up too and hugged Zulmira from behind.

At lunchtime everybody was talking about Ana's departure and when she didn't come for lunch, the girls were disappointed. They all wanted to know what Ana was going to do when she left the "easy life" behind.

'I bet she'll open a shoe shop,' Pequena guessed. 'She loves shoes. She's got four pairs!'

'Maybe Indio gave her enough money to buy a smallholding,' Carmem said.

'It's possible. He is very stupid,' Cloé said, laughing. 'I'm warning you, when Ana leaves he is mine.'

'Cloé, I thought you didn't lay with native Indians and black people,' Carmem said.

'I don't like them but if they have the money...' Cloé responded, realizing, too late, that Zulmira was in the kitchen.

Zulmira stared at Cloé. Everyone watched Cloé swallowing her food while her face went pale. Zulmira continued to stare at her and when Cloé pushed her plate forward and stormed out of the kitchen they were relieved.

'Where's Ana then?' Pequena asked, as if nothing had happened.

'She went to Mina Dourada to say goodbye to some of the boys,' Murilo said. 'Dona Branca said she could go, if she was back before dinner tonight.'

In the evening, when Ana came for dinner, everyone was waiting for her to hear the news.

'Sit next to me, Ana.' Pequena tapped on the chair next to her.

'Did Indio give you the money to go home for good then?' Murilo asked.

'Yes,' Ana confirmed. 'He's giving me enough to buy my parents' old bakery shop.'

'I never knew your parents had a bakery shop,' Carmem said.

'They used to own a bakery shop when I was a child, but they sold it.'

'If they were that rich why did you end up here then?' Cloé asked.

'Shut up, Cloé!' Murilo frowned at Cloé.

Ana took a long and deep breath while everyone stared at her. 'Don't worry, Murilo.' The sadness in her voice was obvious to everyone. 'It was a long time ago.'

'We'll miss you very much, Ana,' Branquinha said in an attempt to change the subject.

'Will you write to us?' Pequena asked Ana. 'I can read now.'

'Of course I will.' Ana smiled. 'And I'll send photos as well.'

'In your baker's uniform?' Pequena smiled back at Ana.

'I hope you've got someone to watch the bread for you or the whole town will have burnt bread,' Zulmira teased Ana.

'I only burnt the beans once, Zulmira!' Ana laughed. 'And only because the pressure cooker stopped working.'

'I wouldn't mind if the beans were burnt every day.' Pequena twisted her mouth. 'I only eat them because Zulmira makes me.'

'Beans are good for you Pequena.' Ana looked at Pequena smiling. 'They make you stronger.'

On the evening of the party, many of Ana's clients came to town. Most of them brought her a gram or two of gold dust carefully weighed and kept in small plastic containers.

'I hope you don't ever need to sell it but if you do, make sure they pay you a fair price.' One of the miners brought Ana a chain. 'It's good gold.'

'Thank you very much. I hope I'll never need to sell it.' Ana closed the clasp of the chain behind her neck and hugged the miner.

Carmem, who had been rehearsing a farewell song, sang it so beautifully that it made a few people cry and Ana was sad to leave so many good friends behind.

At the end of the night, when most of the girls had retired to their rooms, Murilo and Dona Branca were counting the money made in the evening.

'It was a really good night, wasn't it?' Murilo said to Dona Branca. 'Are you going to give ten per cent to Ana?'

'Of course, Murilo. Ana is a good girl who has suffered enough.' Dona Branca put the money in her pocket. 'If she is going to succeed, she needs all the help she can get.'

'So what is Ana's story then?' Cloé, who was still waiting for her last client, asked Dona Branca and Murilo.

'When Ana was fifteen she got pregnant. When her father found out he beat her so badly that she almost died, then he threw her out of the house,' Murilo said.

'The neighbours heard and called the nuns, who took her in and looked after her until she had the baby,' Dona Branca explained.

'The beating was so bad that the baby was born with severe learning problems.' Dona Branca walked closer to Cloé. 'She didn't give up on the baby though. After the girl was born, she couldn't care for the little one and herself,' Dona Branca went on, 'so she turned to this life.'

'Every month she sends money to the woman who looks after her child.' Murilo nodded in approval. 'The girl is fourteen now but she has the brain of a baby and is good for nothing,' Murilo finished.

Cloé didn't reply. Instead she took a wad of notes from her pocket and gave it to Dona Branca. 'Include this with the money you're giving to Ana'. Cloé poured herself a drink of whisky and lifting the glass to Murilo, she said, 'Add this to my account.' She went outside to wait for her last punter.

On the Monday morning everyone got up early to say goodbye to Ana. They all wished her good luck and Pequena gave her a drawing of a bakery and a tall lady wearing a pink apron.

'I know your apron will be white, but I know you like pink too.'

While Murilo placed Ana's suitcases in the wheelbarrow they had borrowed from Seu Mineiro, Ana said goodbye to her friends.

'Write to us,' Carmem reminded her.

With Murilo pushing the wheelbarrow and Branquinha helping him when it got stuck in one of the holes on the ground they made their way to the old VW van which would take Ana to the coach station in Moraes de Almeida.

'I'm going to buy you some sweets for your trip,' Pequena said, running away towards the little kiosk which sold everything from large white knickers to mints and cigarettes.

'I wanted to tell you something but I didn't want to say it in front of everyone.' Ana looked at Murilo and Branquinha. 'I'm going

126

home because I'm pregnant.' She had tears in her eyes.

'So the story about the bakery isn't true then?' Murilo seemed apprehensive.

'How are you going to support your daughter and the baby if you are going home, Ana?' Branquinha said, very concerned.

'Oh, don't worry,' Ana reassured them. 'Indio did give me enough to buy the bakery. Things have changed and now that my father has died my family will welcome me.'

'You got me worried there, sister!' Murilo placed his hand on his heart while Branquinha smiled in relief.

'They will last you a while.' Pequena returned with a bag full of hard-boiled sweets and gave them to Ana.

'The car is here.' Murilo hurried them.

With her case in the luggage compartment on top of the van, Ana climbed on the car and, turning around, she waved goodbye.

A few minutes later, Ana's mud-covered van left Jardim do Ouro.

Branquinha, Murilo and Pequena waved, hoping Ana would never come back.

The Rash

Branquinha and Pequena were sitting in the salon.

'You need to pay more attention when you write in pen, Pequena. You can't erase it like you can in pencil.'

'I don't know why I have to copy this in pen. You let me use a pencil when I do my sums.' Pequena put the pen in her mouth.

'You are allowed to use pencils when doing sums because you need to be very precise when writing numbers so you never get them wrong. Also, it's not as easy to cross them out if you make a mistake when you are doing sums.'

'Ah... but I still don't see the problem of copying this in pencil.'

'Pequena, take that pen out of your mouth, stop talking and concentrate on copying the story.'

'OK, bossy boots.' Pequena carried on with her writing for half a minute before lifting her head to ask, 'Are you writing to your mum again?'

'Pequena!' Branquinha told the younger girl off.

The silence didn't last long as Jandaia came in and sat down. 'Hello.'

'Good morning, Jandaia.' Pequena smiled.

'Pequena, the sooner you do that copying, the quicker you can go.' Branquinha put her pen down.

'I don't know why you make me copy stories I don't like.'

'You have to read things you don't like so you know what you like. Or how would you know you don't like it if you haven't read it?' Branquinha asked the younger girl.

'But I've already read it.' Pequena was not happy. 'Why do you make me copy these stories? The words are so long and difficult.'

'Pequena, if you want to learn to write well, you need to learn to spell difficult words,' Branquinha replied.

'Yeah, Pequena, you can write a letter to your mother and tell her that you can now read and write well, including long and difficult words,' Jandaia said in her soothing voice.

'Oh yes, my mum'd like that.' A few minutes later Pequena finished copying the story, packed her things and left the room.

'You OK?' Branquinha sensed Jandaia was not quite all right.

'I have a problem and I don't know what to do.' Jandaia looked down to the rough wooden floor.

'What's wrong Jandaia?'

'I have a funny rash.'

'Oh. Have you put some rash ointment on it?'

'I can't because the rash ointment instructions say not to put any... uhm... down there.' Jandaia twisted her hands on her lap.

'Oh, I see,' Branquinha replied, not knowing what to say. 'Go and see Seu Geraldo; he'll give you something for it.'

'I'm embarrassed.' Jandaia was still avoiding Branquinha's eyes.

'Don't be silly. I'll come with you.' Branquinha put her hand on the other girl's hand, 'Go and get some money while I finish this letter.'

As per usual Seu Geraldo was very helpful. 'Wash the area with baby soap, dry it well and apply this lotion three times a day. It's expensive, but it will heal the skin in a few days.'

'Thank you, Seu Geraldo.' Jandaia had kept her sunglasses on throughout the appointment.

'And don't have intercourse with anyone for at least a week or you'll pass it on to them,' Seu Geraldo advised before they left.

'How am I going to tell Dona Branca?' Jandaia asked Branquinha when they got back.

'I know. She's not going to be happy and you'll have to pay a big fine.'

'A fine?' Jandaia looked at Branquinha. 'What do you mean by a fine?'

'Did Murilo not tell you?'

'Tell me what, Branquinha?'

'You have one day off a week and if you don't work the other days you have to pay a fine unless you are having your period.'

'Oh my god, I didn't know anything about fines. I haven't got enough money. I'm still paying the van driver who brought me here.' Jandaia couldn't hold back the tears.

'I didn't realise Carmem had to pay a fine when she was in hospital.'

'Dona Branca waived the fee that time,' Branquinha explained.

'Oh my god, what am I going to do? How am I going to be able to send money to my children this month if I can't have clients and on top of everything I have to pay a fine?'

'Just give it a bit of time, Jandaia.' Branquinha put her arms around the other girl. 'Things will be all right.'

'What's the matter Jandaia?' Neither Branquinha nor Jandaia had heard Dona Branca coming into the salon. 'Why are you crying, my child?'

'I have...'

'Jandaia has a very bad period pain, Dona Branca, and nearly fainted earlier.' Branquinha interrupted Jandaia. 'We went to see Seu Geraldo and he gave her some medicine.'

'Didn't you have your period the other day, Jandaia?' Dona Branca put her hands on her hips.

'It came again, but Seu Geraldo gave her some medication to help her out with that too,' Branquinha replied on Jandaia's behalf.

Dona Branca stared at Jandaia and Branquinha for a few seconds before she said to Branquinha, 'Father Domingos asked me to give you this.' She took an envelope from her pocket and gave it to Branquinha.

As she walked towards the door, she turned round and said to Jandaia, 'You'd better sort this out because I can't afford keeping girls who have two periods in a month!'

The Letter

Branquinha stared at the yellow and green stripes on the edge of the envelope. As she tore it open, there were two pieces of paper neatly folded.

She unfolded them, hoping they were the news she was waiting for.

Moraes de Almeida, Pará, 3rd January

> *Dona Lucinda,*
> *I received a letter from Father Bento from the Church in Bragantina this morning and I had it copied word for word because I feel it is relevant to you.*
> *With the blessings of Our Lord Jesus Christ*
> *Father Domingos*

Branquinha breathed deeply and looked at the neatly typed letter.

Bragantina, Paraná, 12th December

> *Dear Reverend Father Domingos,*
> *It was a great pleasure to receive news from you and to learn you are well and alive, fighting our Lord's cause in such a distant and unhospitable land.*
> *I have made enquires about the lady you wrote me about and I am fairly certain I have found her family.*
> *If I am right in my assumptions, her name is not Rita (or Ritinha)*

but Maria Rita Gomes. Maria Rita was born on the same date you gave me and her mother was also called Ines. In my opinion, this is too much of a coincidence not to be the same person.

Maria Rita Gomes was a nurse in the local hospital. She disappeared from Bragantina eight years ago after she was accused of killing her grandmother. I never met Maria Rita but upon receiving your letter I visited the family and they told me that the grandmother was very ill and in terrible pain begging everyone to end her life. As we know, Satan works in evil ways and Maria Rita was not able to fight him and ended the grandmother's pain by smothering her with a pillow.

Nobody would have suspected anything about the death if it was not for her sister-in-law coming into the room and witnessing the event.

Her family, however, has forgiven her and they have been looking for Maria Rita's whereabouts for quite some time.

If the deceased young woman is proven to be Maria Rita, I would like to be the bearer of the news to the family. Also, I beg you to not tell them that she lost her way in life. Her mother is unwell and will not be with us for much longer.

Please let me know if I can be of further help.

Your brother in faith,

Father Bento

Branquinha put the letters back in the envelope and went to the kitchen.

'Zulmira, you need to see this. And where is Murilo?'

'He went to the gold trading shop to send money to pay for the new stereo.' Zulmira was cutting onions and had tears in her eyes. 'What is it, Branquinha?'

'Father Domingos sent me a letter he received from the priest in Bragantina.'

Zulmira looked at her with a blank face.

'Remember I went to see Father Domingos to ask for help to find Ritinha's family in Bragantina?'

'Oh my god, I remember now.' Zulmira's eyes opened wider. 'Has he found anything?'

'Yes, he has.' Branquinha pulled the envelope out of her pocket. 'The priest in Bragantina is sure he has found her family. There's this girl called Maria Rita Gomes with the same date of birth and her mother is called Ines.'

'I can't believe it, Branquinha.' Zulmira washed her hands and dried them. 'Let me read it.'

Branquinha took the letters from the envelope and gave them to Zulmira.

'Oh my god, she was a nurse...' Zulmira was crying again.

News that they had found Ritinha's family soon spread and opinion on what to do next was divided.

'There's no way the family will not realise that she was living an "easy" life,' Carmem said.

'We don't need to tell them,' Branquinha argued.

'They'll take one look at our lot and they'll know she was a whore,' Cloé laughed.

'We could tell them she was a nurse,' Pequena suggested.

'Don't be stupid, Pequena. A nurse living in a whorehouse! Who would believe it?' Cloé replied.

'No! That's not a bad idea, Pequena.' Murilo got up. 'Ritinha was a great nurse.' He stepped down from the porch and walked across the street to Seu Geraldo's pharmacy.

Patient Confidentiality

India Rosa came on a visit and told everyone how two of João Preto's men had a rash on their private parts. 'They must have caught it from the same woman,' she said.

Jandaia looked at Branquinha, worried.

'Not from anyone here,' Murilo replied. 'Our girls are all clean.'

'They probably picked it up from one of Eugenia Brothel's women,' Dona Branca said crossing the room and sitting near India Rosa. 'I heard they had a bad case of scabies as well as nits, and that the house is infested with fleas.'

'I wouldn't be surprised if they caught it from them either,' Murilo said scratching his head. 'When my friend worked there he constantly had to have his head sprayed with cucaracha's poison because of all the headlice.'

'Jandaia,' Cloé called loudly from the table across the salon, 'didn't you sleep with them when they were here last time?'

Branquinha saw Jandaia's face going pale behind her sunglasses.

'I don't know who you mean...'

'They didn't catch anything from Jandaia. She had her period three times this month!' Dona Branca interrupted. 'Where are the miners now?' Dona Branca asked India Rosa.

'They are with Seu Geraldo,' India Rosa answered.

'I'll go and have a word with them.' Dona Branca stood up and crossed the road.

It didn't take long for Dona Branca to come back. 'It's not from here,' she told everyone. 'Seu Geraldo said the boys must have caught it over two to three months ago because their skin has come off,

134

leaving the flesh exposed.'

'And now the whole village knows about their skinless itchy cocks.' Murilo laughed, swinging on the back legs of his chairs, his feet pushing the banister. 'So much for patient privacy and confidentiality!'

'Maybe they caught it from each other,' Dona Branca said, and everyone laughed.

Jandaia's secret was safe.

A Good Woman

'Ana wrote us a letter,' Dona Branca said as she sat down at the head of the table at lunchtime.

Murilo and the girls looked at Dona Branca and before anyone asked a question she put her hand in her pocket and pulled out a letter and placed it on the table next to her plate.

'I'll read it when we finish lunch,' Dona Branca said before she ate a mouthful of butternut squash and rice.

Afterwards, Zulmira cleared the plates and pans away and wiped the table before sitting down again to hear Dona Branca reading the letter.

Goiania, 16th January
My dear friends
You have no idea just how much I miss everyone.

Life has been very tough here with a lot of work. The money I brought with me was not quite enough to buy the bakery but the owner accepted my offer to pay for it in instalments and I have managed to make all the payments without being late. Dona Branca, the extra money you sent me last month couldn't have arrived at a better time.

They started building an estate not far from my bakery and it has been a godsend. About fifty families moved in so far and most of them have children and we all know how much bread and cake children eat.

One of the boys who works here suggested we also make pizza and although initially I was a bit hesitant I agreed to give it a trial and what a good idea it was! We now sell more pizza than bread on Saturdays and Sundays.

The cakes are going well, too. I put a couple of display cakes on the window and since then they have been selling so well.

I miss you all and I know you must miss me too. Please, if any of you come to Goiania come to visit, but remember, I'm now a very respectable shopkeeper.

Give my regards to everyone.

Lots of love,

Ana

'So you were wrong then, Dona Branca,' Pequena pointed out.

Dona Branca, lowered her glasses on her nose and looked at the young girl. 'And I have never been so happy in being "wrong", Pequena. Ana is a wonderful woman who deserves a break.' She stood up and before walking out of the room she turned around and said, 'I hope that, soon, you will all find a good path and leave this life too.'

Everyone sat quiet reflecting on what Dona Branca had wished upon them, realising what a good woman Dona Branca really was.

After that conversation, Branquinha was curious to know how Dona Branca had ended up running a place like Casa da Branca. 'Do you know how it happened?' Branquinha asked Murilo when she was helping him washing the glasses in the evening.

'She doesn't talk much about it, but I heard her telling Zulmira one day,' Murilo replied. 'Her husband was a drug addict and ran into a lot of debt with the local drug dealer. The dealer wanted Branca's house in lieu of the debt, but Branca managed to persuade him to let her run his brothel and pay her husband's debt.'

'What happened to the husband?' Branquinha asked.

'When the dealer came for his money he ran away leaving Branca with two young children. She brought up the two kids on her own. Gui turned out to be a nasty piece of shit like his father, but her daughter is a teacher and a good girl.'

Dijé

'Dijé got a shipment of chocolate today,' Pequena said to Carmem and Branquinha. 'Let's go and get some before it all gets sold out.'

The girls left the Casa da Branca and crossed the road towards Restaurante da Dijé.

'Good afternoon, girls!' Branquinha could swear that Dijé, the light-brown lady who ran the restaurant, had a permanent smile on her face.

'We heard you got some chocolate today,' Pequena said to Dijé. 'Have you got any Garoto chocolate?'

Dijé's smile got even bigger and she leaned behind the counter to reach for a yellow box of chocolates. 'Is this what you mean?' she asked placing a box in front of Pequena.

'How many have you got?' Pequena asked Dijé. 'I haven't had chocolate for more than... it must be two months now.'

'I've got five boxes, but I want to share it with other people. We have not had any chocolate since you bought the last box at Christmas, so today I can only sell you one box.' Dijé smiled again. 'But I also got a new ice cream machine and I made some sweetcorn ice cream if you would like to try some.'

Carmem, whose weight had reduced considerably since the ice cream parlour closed, jumped and said '*Guapa*, I'll have three scoops!'

Dijé laughed. 'Take a seat and I'll bring it to you in a minute.'

'Carmem, why do you like ice cream so much?' Pequena asked as they sat down at a table in the corner.

'I don't like all ice creams,' Carmem replied. 'I like sweetcorn ice cream because when I lived in Paraguay I had not even heard of it.'

The girls were enjoying their ice cream when a short, well-fed lady walked in. Branquinha recognised her; she was the lady who had called her a harlot at the church in Mores de Almeida.

'Good afternoon, Dona Socorro.' The girls heard Dijé greeting the woman. 'How can I help you today?'

'I heard you got some chocolate in. I will have all the boxes of chocolate you still have,' the lady said.

'I can only sell you one box because I want to share among the villagers,' Dijé said, and again, she was smiling. 'I have sweetcorn ice cream, though,' Dijé added. 'Would you like some?'

'And you expect me to sit in the same room as those whores?' Dona Socorro replied, nodding toward Branquinha, Carmem and Pequena.

'Dona Socorro,' Dijé said calmly, 'perhaps you would like to take some ice cream home with you instead?'

'Why do I have to go home with my ice cream? Why don't you send those harlots home with *their* ice creams?' Dona Socorro spoke loudly enough to attract the attention of some people who were outside the building. 'You've always served these women in your establishment but it's time for you to stop it.'

Carmem stood up, ready to leave but Dijé held her hand up, stopping them, and mouthed, 'Stay!'

'Dona Socorro, please?' Dijé tried to appease the woman. 'These girls help me make my living.'

A small crowd had quickly gathered at the wide-open doors, spilling into the restaurant. Everyone wanting to see what the "show" was all about.

'Let them crawl back to the hole they came from!' The bigger the crowd became, the louder Dona Socorro spoke.

'Everyone's welcome in my restaurant, regardless of their profession.' Dijé's smile was still there, but slightly faded and it no longer reached her eyes.

'Since when was opening your legs to men for money a profession?'

'Dona Socorro, please.' Dijé raised her voice ever so slightly and for the first time people saw Dijé without a smile on her face.

'You have not heard me!' Dona Socorro came closer to Dijé. 'I will ask again. Since when is opening your legs to men for money a profession?'

'I did hear you, Dona Socorro, but now that you demand an answer, I'll give you one.' Dijé's face was pale and her voice faltering. 'Isn't opening your legs to a man exactly what you do with your husband?'

Dona Socorro's fat face went redder. 'What?' she shouted.

'You slag your husband off day after day saying you despise him and how disgusting he is.' Dijé went on, 'You tell everyone how awful it is to have sex with him and that you only do that because you need him to pay the bills.'

'I'm a married woman!' Dona Socorro shouted again.

'But what is your profession exactly, Dona Socorro?' Dijé asked. 'I'd say, it is to open your legs for money! Don't you think so?'

The crowd didn't wait for Dona Socorro's answer before they all burst all burst out laughing.

Dona Socorro didn't reply and, as she started moving towards the door, Dijé called, 'Dona Socorro, please pay for the chocolates! If there's one type of person I won't tolerate on my premises, it's a thief!'

Dona Socorro threw the box of chocolate on the floor and left the restaurant.

'Sweetcorn ice cream, anyone?' Dijé shouted to the crowd. She was smiling again.

The Table Runner

The rainy season was a long one and when Pedro, the lorry driver, arrived, driving the first lorry full of provisions in early April, they all cheered. Pedro's truck was part of a caravan of eight lorries, which were all covered in mud. The trucks parked in line along the road, waiting to cross the River Jamanxim on the ferry, one at the time.

'Never seen it so wet,' Pedro told them. 'The mud lakes were the biggest ones I've ever seen. Some of them were half a kilometre long and others were so deep that we had to avoid them or it would swallow the lorry. It took me over twenty days to drive the last four hundred kilometres and only managed to get here because we had a tractor travelling with us.'

'How long until they start bringing cows up the road?' Branquinha asked hoping no one noticed her anxiety.

'Not for another month or so. It's too wet,' Pedro explained. 'Is Pequena around? Her cousin asked me to give her a letter.'

They all looked worried. Pequena never received letters and the only person who knew where to find her was a cousin.

Your father passed away three weeks ago. Your mother needs you home, Soraia', the letter said.

'Who is Soraia?' Jandaia whispered to Branquinha.

'It's Pequena's name,' Branquinha replied.

Pequena didn't cry and everyone understood why. Pedro told Pequena she could go back in the lorry with him when he returned a week later, but Pequena knew that going back to her mother's home was no longer an option, and instead, she asked Pedro if he could give her mother a packet on his way back.

In the next few days Pequena worked hard on her crochet and by the time Pedro came back she had a nice table runner for her mum.

Branquinha and Jandaia helped Pequena wrap the parcel.

'My mum will be so happy that I've learned to read and write. I'll put the envelope with the letter and the money in the folded table runner,' Pequena said.

'Why doesn't she send the money via the gold trading shop?' Jandaia asked Branquinha.

'Pequena's family think she is in a convent. If she sends the money via the gold trading shop they will send her mother a bank order and she'll know she is not living in a convent but in a mining area,' Branquinha explained.

A few hours later, Pequena gave the parcel to Pedro. 'Please don't tell her I'm here.'

'I won't,' Pedro promised. 'I'll say one of the nuns in São Paulo knew I was passing by the village where your mum lives and asked me to bring the parcel with me.'

'Why didn't you want to go back home to see your family?' Branquinha heard Jandaia asking Pequena while they all watched Pedro's lorry disappear in the distance.

'I'll only leave this place when Martinho comes for me.'

Branquinha smiled. She knew it was just a matter of time for Pequena's life to take shape...

Ritinha's Secret

'That is a nice car.' Pequena pointed to a red pick-up truck driving down the road and parking outside Seu Geraldo's pharmacy.

'It is!' Murilo squinted his eyes. 'I wonder why he is not queuing for the ferry. The ferry is leaving soon.'

'How weird,' Carmem said. 'Maybe they are related to Seu Geraldo. Nobody stops in this godforsaken village unless they have to!'

They watched a tall man in jeans and a blue shirt get out of the car, followed by a woman wearing beige trousers and a white blouse with high-heeled shoes on her feet.

'Where does she think she's going to?' Murilo frowned. 'The nearest fashion show is in Eugenia's Brothel.'

Everyone laughed and when the truck turned around, in the direction of Moraes de Almeida, they saw Seu Geraldo crossing the road.

'That was Ritinha's brother and his wife,' Seu Geraldo explained. 'They're taking her body home.'

'Oh my god... What did you tell them?' Murilo asked.

'I told them Ritinha worked for me and slept in one of the rooms at the back'.

Do you think they believed our story?'

'I think they did.'

'Why did they go back to Moraes de Almeida then?' Branquinha asked.

'They want Father Domingos to be present to bless the body.' Seu Geraldo wiped the sweat from his forehead with a white handkerchief.

'The body will be decomposed by now.' Murilo sounded apprehensive. 'She died over a year ago.'

'They brought a special coffin with them,' Seu Geraldo explained. 'They asked me if I could find a couple of people to do the digging.'

'I'll get that sorted out.' Murilo jumped off the banister and headed up the road in search of some grave-diggers.

A few hours later, scarves wrapped around their faces, half of the people living in Jardim do Ouro were all gathered in the cemetery.

Sergeant Armando, having signed off all the paperwork confirming that the man was a legitimate relative of the deceased, stood looking important by the tomb.

'Poor Ritinha,' Carmem whispered to Branquinha, 'to be disturbed from her grave like that.'

'She's going home,' Branquinha whispered back. 'She's going to be near her mother.'

After a while, the men managed to break into the concrete tomb above the grave and began to dig. They had not been digging long when it started raining and everyone ran for cover. The show was not worth getting wet for.

'Carry on digging,' the brother said to the diggers when they wanted to stop too. 'I'll pay double.'

Murilo sat on the ground, cold with his arms wrapped around his knees, his shirt stuck to his body, wet, standing guard next to Ritinha's grave while the two men worked their way down the hole.

The rain made the soil softer but heavier to lift up.

The brother sat in the car with the sister-in-law looking through a magazine, bored. Occasionally they would wind the window down and smoke a cigarette.

It took a long time to bring the coffin up and, by the time they managed to, the rain had stopped and the villagers were back.

Ritinha's brother, using a crowbar, prised the coffin lid open.

'Oh my god!' Murilo cried, falling on his knees.

'Our Lady Maria Aparecida pray for us!' Zulmira blessed herself with the sign of the cross.

Branquinha looked inside the coffin and saw Ritinha's pale face as if she was asleep.

144

'In the name of the father, the son and the holy ghost...' Father Domingos blessed the body. 'Don't be afraid, my children. God's ways are often mysterious. Sometimes this happens and the body does not decay.'

Seu Geraldo quickly closed the coffin and soon the body was moved to his pharmacy where it was transferred to the newer coffin and then taken to the church for the final blessing.

Everyone from the Casa da Branca came to the mass and sat on the front benches.

'You are all from the brothel across the road.' Ritinha's sister-in-law walked towards them. 'You have no place sitting here,' she said.

'We all knew Ritinha. She was our friend,' Murilo answered quietly.

'She wasn't your friend,' the woman replied. 'She was a nurse doing her job.'

'She lived...'

'Shush, Pequena.' Dona Branca interrupted the young girl.

'Ritinha helped many of us when we were ill,' Murilo tried again.

'No. We don't want you here. Please leave!' the woman insisted.

'Let him who is without sin cast the first stone.' They heard Father Domingos from the pulpit. 'This is a house of God and everyone is welcome.'

The sister-in-law didn't reply. She walked away towards her husband while Father Domingos stood silent in the same place until the sister-in-law was on the other side of the room.

That night, Dona Branca didn't open the brothel and people sat in the salon playing cards, unusually quiet. They were all sad but at the same time pleased that Ritinha had gone home to her mother and her secret was safe.

Gringo Returns

G ringo had been to Casa da Branca three times that week.

'So glad the wet season is over,' Murilo said to Gringo, placing a glass and a bottle of Gringo's favourite whisky on the table. 'Branquinha is in the shower. She'll be here soon.'

'I thought Branquinha wasn't allowed to see Gringo,' Pequena said to Murilo.

'She is when Cloé is away.' Murilo wiped the counter.

'Ah! And what will happen when Cloé comes back?'

'I guess Branquinha is not going to stay here forever.'

'When do you think she is going then?'

'How do I know, Pequena?' Murilo threw his cloth in the bowl, splashing water everywhere. 'Why don't you go and tell Branquinha to hurry up from that shower?'

Gringo was lying in bed, his head resting on his arm, smoking and watching Branquinha drying the ends of her hair that had been caught under the shower.

'Let me comb it for you.' Gringo placed the half-smoked cigarette into an empty can of coke, taking the comb from the bedside table, and he gently started combing Branquinha's hair.

'My hair is going to smell of cigarette now,' Branquinha complained to Gringo. 'You should stop smoking. It's a stupid habit.'

'I know, but I haven't got a TV or a wife to keep me distracted.' Gringo laughed.

'You should be a hairdresser,' Branquinha said as he combed her hair.

'I did consider that when I was about fourteen and my friend and

146

I were thinking which jobs would give us the best chances to touch girls.' Gringo chuckled.

'If that was your plan, I think you ended up in the wrong profession and at the wrong place.' Branquinha laughed back. 'How did you end up here anyway?'

'I was visiting Manaus and met a Belgian pilot who needed someone to take pictures for him,' Gringo said while untangling Branquinha's hair.

'Were you a photographer then?'

'No, but I had a good camera.' Gringo laughed at his own joke, his white teeth straight and strong.

'But Manaus is so far from here.'

'The pilot was coming this way and I hooked up with him and ended up down here,' Gringo explained. 'It is a crazy place.'

Branquinha didn't reply.

'You told me you came to get money for your mother's treatment, but why are you still here?' Gringo gathered Branquinha's hair together and wound the elastic band around it.

'I figured out that going back when I had enough money for my mum's treatment would not solve my problems. It would be just a matter of time until I would find myself in the same hole again.'

'That's a good point. So what are you saving up for, then?' Gringo put the comb down and sat back in the bed.

'Murilo suggested I should start a chicken farm,' Branquinha replied. 'He is quite smart when it comes to money.'

'Yeah, Murilo is no fool.'

'What about you? Why are you still here? What are you planning for your life?'

Gringo didn't answer. He pushed Branquinha to the middle of the bed and lay on top of her, changing the subject.

Branquinha had learnt her place. She gave him what he was paying for and asked no more questions.

A while after Gringo had finished and Branquinha was half asleep he answered her. 'I'm here for the adventure, Branquinha. I don't have a plan.'

The Day Off

Branquinha woke up before Gringo and went to the bathroom next door to have a shower. She liked staying in the hotel with him, but she missed her toiletries and her own towels.

'What are you doing today?' Gringo asked Branquinha when she got back to the bedroom.

'Nothing much... maybe teach Pequena about the solar system.'

'How come you are so well educated?' Gringo stared at Branquinha, his blue eyes shadowed by his dark eyelashes.

Branquinha laughed. 'I'm not well educated. People learn about the solar system in school when they are still young.'

'You are more educated than most people here. How much schooling did you have?' Gringo put a folded pillow behind Branquinha's head and pulled the white cotton sheet over her breast.

'I stopped when I was eighteen.' Branquinha adjusted the pillow behind her neck. 'When I finished secondary school.'

'Why didn't you go to university?' Gringo lit a cigarette.

'I wanted to but there was no way I could leave my mother all by herself and go to a big city to study.' Branquinha sat up a little higher in bed. 'But I don't mind...'

'You are clever. You should give it a go.' Gringo rolled over and lay on his folded arm.

'I will if I win the lottery.' Branquinha laughed and jumped out of bed. 'You asked me what I was doing today. What are you doing today?'

'I was thinking of taking a certain lady to see some butterflies I wanted to photograph.' Gringo smiled at Branquinha. 'Would you like to come with me?'

Gringo and Branquinha crossed on the ferry and drove about five miles down the dirt track; the overgrown trees on the side of the road hung above the pick-up truck.

'Why do you have to come this far just to see butterflies?' Branquinha asked Gringo.

'Because they are the most beautiful creatures you'll ever see and you can only see them here,' he replied. 'There are very few places in the world that have butterflies as striking as the ones in the Amazon.'

Gringo parked the car by the road near a spring and, taking his camera bag from behind his seat, he and Branquinha walked towards the water.

'Watch your step,' Gringo warned Branquinha. 'Snakes don't live near water but there are many holes on the ground and you can hurt yourself if you lose your foot.'

As they approached the waterside a cloud of bright and colourful butterflies flew from the edge towards Branquinha.

'Oh my god, I see what you mean!' Branquinha shouted above the whirring of the thousand butterflies dancing around her. 'They are incredible.'

'They are amazing, aren't they?' Gringo said, setting his camera on a tripod.

For a while they sat next to the river, under a small tree and Branquinha watched Gringo take pictures of all sorts of insects.

'Maybe you should get rid of your cigarette. Don't you know insects don't like smoke?' Branquinha giggled across the spring.

At lunchtime they ate the snacks Gringo had brought from Dijé's Restaurant and in the afternoon they walked into the forest and he showed her his favourite butterfly.

'I've never managed to take a picture of it because it flies too fast.' Gringo pointed to a large, blue butterfly jazzing through the green foliage of the forest.

When Gringo and Branquinha went back to the house in the afternoon, she was glad Murilo wasn't there. She didn't want a lecture after such a perfect day.

Come With Me...

It was Gringo's last day in town. He had paid for Branquinha full time in advance and had organized an extra house fee with Murilo. 'Come with me to my camp for a few days,' Gringo said to Branquinha.

'I can't,' Branquinha replied. 'If I come with you, I'll have to pay a fine to Dona Branca.'

'What do you mean a fine? She can't hold you prisoner here!' Gringo's accent got heavier when he was angry.

'I know I'm not a prisoner! I can leave any time I want, but if I do, there might not be room for me when I get back,' Branquinha explained. 'When Gigi left she had to live in a shed for weeks before she moved back here.'

'You don't need to come back here, if you don't want to.' Gringo held his arms around Branquinha's waist. 'You can stay with me.'

Branquinha avoided his eyes. She didn't want to lie to Gringo, but she couldn't bring herself to tell him that her heart belonged to another man and that she was waiting for him to come back for her. She leant over and reached for her dress.

'Think about it and let me know next time I'm around,' Gringo said, buttoning his shirt up. 'Meanwhile, if you change your mind, you know where to find me.' He left the room, shutting the door behind him.

'I told you this was going to get complicated,' Murilo said to Branquinha. 'What are you going to say when Cloé gets back?'

Carmem and Pequena looked at Branquinha, waiting for an answer.

'I don't have to say anything.'

'Get real, Branquinha!' Murilo had his hands on his hips, his new black leather jacket catching the light coming from the outside. 'I'm sorry I stole your best client while you were away, Cloé,' Murilo mimed Branquinha's voice, 'and by the way, he asked me to move in with him.'

'She didn't steal anyone from Cloé,' Carmem said to Murilo.

'Sister, you are in shit. Shit! Shit! Shit!' Murilo ignored Carmem's attempt to defend Branquinha. 'Dona Branca sent money for Cloé's plane fare and she'll be here next week. Be prepared.'

As Murilo walked off towards the back of the house, Pequena, Carmem and Branquinha sat in the salon, quietly.

'Don't worry too much about it, Branquinha.' Pequena got up and tapped Branquinha on the shoulder. 'I think no one will tell Cloé because she is such a bitch and nobody likes her.'

Branquinha spent the next few days asking herself if she had done the right thing and wondering if Cloé would find out.

A week later, Cloé arrived. They were all in the salon looking at the presents she had brought for Dona Branca and Zulmira.

'This is for you,' Cloé said to Pequena, throwing her a red hairbrush. 'Don't get used to presents. I only bought it because it was cheap.'

'And what is this bag?' Murilo peered into a carrier bag.

'Leave it alone.' Cloé slapped Murilo's hand. 'That is for Gringo.'

'Ah...' Murilo gave the bag back to Cloé.

'Has he been here then?' she asked, looking at Branquinha.

'Uhm...'

'Yes, a few times,' Murilo replied.

Branquinha held her breath.

'He had a whisky, asked about you, but didn't stay.' He looked Cloé in the eye. 'I guess our girls are just not his type.'

The Wrong Time of the Month

It was Branquinha's time of the month and she was lucky that her period only lasted three days. Branquinha kept her room cleaned and tidy and there was not much more to do during her time off so that morning she decided to help Murilo clean the freezer.

'You are blessed, *guapa*,' Carmem said to Branquinha. 'My period lasts for at least five days and sometimes longer. I don't understand why Dona Branca doesn't let us do it during our menstruation.'

'It's because it is bad for business!' Murilo lifted his head from inside the freezer and shouted, 'And it's dirty, so stop talking about it before you put any arriving customer off.'

'Still can't see the point...' Carmem continued but was interrupted by Cloé's arrival.

'Murilo, Gringo is in town,' she said short of breath. 'I'm going to have a shower and when he comes in, send him straight to my room.'

'Of course, Cloé,' Murilo responded looking at Branquinha, his pressed lips giving away his feelings.

'You know he is not going to come for Cloé!' Murilo said when the other girl left the room. 'Sister, you and Gringo are going to land us in trouble because you know what she will do if she finds out about your escapades with her xodó!'

'She is delusional, Murilo,' Branquinha whispered. 'Gringo told me he only stayed with Cloé a few times and he never promised her anything!'

'She is delusional all right but to be fair, all women are delusional, that is what makes them women!' Murilo's laughter was interrupted by Gringo's arrival.

The foreigner stood at the door and wiped his forehead, his eyes squinting, adapting to the lack of the bright light which bathed the outside.

'Cloé said for you to go straight to her room.' Murilo bent over the counter looking from the half-open hatch on the wall.

'Thank you, Murilo, but I'm not here to see Cloé.' Gringo walked towards Branquinha. 'I need to go to the bank in Moraes de Almeida and thought you might want to come with me. We could have lunch there and you'll be in time for work this evening.'

'Man, you can't come here and ask Branquinha out when your other woman is at the back showering and dollying herself up for you.' Murilo came out of his room and stood in the salon, his hands on his hips. 'If Cloé finds out you are all dead.'

'Murilo, I don't want to hurt anybody but I have not promised anything to Cloé. I'm sorry she feels that way, but I'm not going to be held ransom to a woman who thinks she has any hold on me.' Gringo's accent was strong, some of his words hard to understand.

'Yes, but what about Branquinha? Cloé is not the type of woman who will forgive anyone who steals her man,' Murilo argued back.

'I understand,' Gringo said to Murilo and then turned to Branquinha. 'If you want to come with me, I'll wait for you up the road.'

Carmem and Murilo looked at Branquinha and when she didn't reply Murilo warned the girl, 'Sister, don't be stupid.'

'You only live once, *guapa*, so go for it.' Carmem stood up and pulled Branquinha off her chair towards the corridor which led to their bedroom. Turning to Gringo, the Paraguayan girl said, 'She'll meet you up the road in twenty minutes.'

Wish Upon a Star

The road which led to Moraes de Almeida was bumpy and slippery. The heavy rain in the previous months soaked the soil and the rivers and springs had overflowed making everything wet and sometimes difficult to pass.

Gringo and Branquinha were sitting in the car while they waited behind a queue of cars waiting for a tractor to put a couple of wide logs across one of the springs so the cars could drive over the water.

Branquinha looked at the lorry which had fallen off the bridge and was now lying sideways in the spring. She wondered how it had happened.

'Probably because it was too heavy and the bridge is too weak or too slippery.' Gringo lit a cigarette. 'Everyone takes so many risks in this place that I'm surprised that more people don't die here.'

Gringo got out of the car and went to ask if he could help, but soon he came back. 'There is nothing we can do but wait. If it was dry we could drive through the spring, but the water is too high this time of the year.'

Branquinha and Gringo sat in the car for a while talking, waiting. She helped him with his pronunciation while he told her about all the many places he had travelled to.

When they finally arrived in Moraes de Almeida it was late afternoon and instead of lunch they had dinner.

'I don't have to go back today.' Slightly embarrassed Branquinha explained to Gringo that she was having her period and she had the time off.

'Why don't you go back to my camp with me then?' Gringo suggested. 'You said you have never been to a mine before. We could stay here tonight and go back in the morning.'

'I didn't bring any clothes.' Branquinha hesitated.

'We could stop at your place on the way back or if you want to avoid going back I'll get you some new ones in the shop here before we leave.' Gringo seemed to have a solution for every problem and Branquinha finally agreed.

On their way back they passed outside Casa da Branca and crossed the ferry, but it was too early for the girls to be awake and no one saw Branquinha sitting in the car with Gringo.

The camp was about an hour and half from Jardim do Ouro. They left the main road and turned into a small trail, the track still full of small plants and Branquinha wondered how the tyres of the pick-up truck managed to drive through the weeded area.

Gringo's hut was covered with a large sheet of black plastic and over it, to keep the heat off, there was a layer of palm tree leaves, all held by a structure of round logs held by the vines men collected from the trees.

Branquinha looked around. Everything was neat and tidy, the beaten soil brushed clean and the colourful hammocks hanging across the hut. She placed her stuff in a corner of the room on top of Gringo's belongings and sat on his hammock, swinging from side to side, enjoying the peace of the forest, the birds singing in the trees and the engine of the machines roaring somewhere in the distance.

'Let's go down the mines and I will show you how we collect the gold,' Gringo said taking Branquinha two hundred metres down a trail to a large clearing in the jungle.

'This is huge,' Branquinha said, pointing to the wide hole of about ten metres by ten and four metres deep. Some of the men were jetting water on the sides of the hole, removing the soil.

'Not really,' Gringo replied. 'I like working on smaller spots. Some miners have much larger pits in the ground.'

'But how do you find the gold?' Branquinha turned to Gringo, covering her eyes from the scorching sun.

'Once the soil is washed, we pump it down there.' Gringo pointed to a leaning structure that resembled a child's slide. 'The mud is then sieved through a few layers of fabric. The gold, which is heavier, sits on the bottom layer. We collect all the soil from that layer in a big tank and throw some mercury into it.'

'Ah...' Branquinha knew about the use of mercury in the extraction of gold.

'The mercury clings to the gold dust, separating it from the sand and once we burn the mercury we have the precious metal.'

'And what happens to all the soil afterwards?' Branquinha wiped the sweat from her forehead.

'Once we leave, the forest will grow over it very fast and in a year or so you will hardly notice we were here.'

'Really?' Branquinha didn't really believe Gringo.

'Can you see that part?' Gringo pointed towards a lower part of the forest. 'I worked that area last year. Give it eight to ten years and even the tall trees will be back.'

'Surely, you don't expect me to think that all this work will not damage the forest permanently.' Branquinha looked at Gringo, her eyes staring into his.

'Babe, don't make me feel guilty!' Gringo replied, helping her up on a fallen tree. 'I'm only doing what everyone here does.'

After dinner – beans, rice and beef stew – the men invited her to play dominoes and once they finished they lay in their hammocks telling each other stories and teasing her about the jaguar that hunted the camp. 'It likes women's flesh better because it is softer,' one of the men said, laughing.

Branquinha wasn't scared until she heard an animal roaring loudly near the camp and when Gringo told her it was a jaguar Branquinha asked to move her hammock nearer to his. The men laughed.

The following day, Branquinha woke up with monkeys screaming above them and birds chirping aloud. As the minutes passed, new creatures woke up, too, claiming their space in the jungle and rejoicing in life.

She got out of the hammock with a sore back and Gringo and the men teased her. 'If you place yourself across the hammock, your body will lay flat and you will sleep better,' Gringo explained.

Branquinha spent the morning reading through Gringo's books – a mixture of English novels and Portuguese language books. 'I didn't realise you actually studied Portuguese,' she said to Gringo.

'I've been living in Brazil for four years.' Gringo shrugged his shoulders. 'I'd better make good use of the opportunity.'

As the only woman in the camp, Branquinha felt obliged to offer to cook and, although Gringo said no to cooking lunch, he allowed her to make pancakes for their afternoon snack.

The rest of the day passed fast. Late afternoon, Gringo grabbed his camera and took Branquinha into the forest to show her some of the largest birds she had heard about, but, because they were shy creatures, people rarely saw them.

'They are toucans.' Gringo passed her the binoculars, pointing to a pair of large blue regal-looking birds on a tree not far from them. 'Their meat is very hard, but people often kill them for their beautiful beaks.'

'And what do they do with the beaks?' Branquinha turned around and looked at Gringo.

'Nothing. Sometimes they use them as decoration or a trophy for a few months until they get bored and throw them away,' Gringo replied pointing his camera towards the bird.

Branquinha felt sick that someone would end the life of such a fine living creature for such a frivolous reason.

In the evening it was the same routine, dominoes, stories and by nine o'clock the men were all snoring stretched across their hammocks.

Gringo, holding Branquinha's hand, took her to his pick-up truck parked a hundred yards or so away from his camp. 'I want to show you something.' Gringo climbed into the back of his truck and laid a blanket on the floor of the car. He helped Branquinha climb up and they lay down staring at the stars.

Branquinha had always loved looking at the stars in the sky late at night when she could see the Southern Cross constellation but what Gringo showed her that night didn't compare with anything she had ever seen. The clear sky was dusted with bright stars, some of them flashing like they were blinking at her.

'When I was little my mum used to tell me that the stars in the sky were children who died while they were young and Jesus turned them into the stars to brighten up the heaven above us.' Branquinha smiled as she told Gringo one of her favourite childhood stories.

'Why have you never married or had children?' Branquinha asked him.

There was a long pause before Gringo replied. 'If I'm going to have children, I have the responsibility to give them a good mother and I've never found anyone good enough who was willing to marry me,' he said, laughing at his own joke.

Branquinha reflected on Gringo's position on fatherhood. 'That is an interesting way of thinking. If more people thought like you, there would be a lot less unhappy people around.'

'Are you planning to have children, Branquinha?' Gringo moved around the blanket.

'I will, when I find a man worthy enough to father my babies,' Branquinha said, immediately regretting it, as she thought about Vilson.

Gringo didn't reply. Instead he carried on smoking his cigarette and counting the stars.

The following day, any connection Branquinha had with Gringo was gone and when he arranged for one of his men to drive her to Jardim do Ouro, Branquinha was relieved.

The Wait

It was a hot and steamy April. Branquinha and Jandaia were sitting on the porch. Jandaia had her feet resting on the banister showing off her brown and smooth legs but still hiding her ugly eyes behind a new pair of large white sunglasses.

'He's on his way, he's on his way!' Branquinha and Jandaia turned around to see Pequena running down the road.

'Who is on his way and why are you shouting?' Branquinha asked.

Pequena, leaning forward, her arms resting on her legs, tried to catch her breath before she spoke, 'They are on their way, not far from here,' she finally managed to say.

'They who?' Jandaia asked.

Pequena took another deep breath. 'The drover and his cows.'

Branquinha felt a wave of warmth wrapping around her body, her brain feeling happy, her mouth smiling, 'Are you sure?'

'Yes,' Pequena replied. 'He didn't see me but I recognised him as the car passed very near him.'

'Oh my god, my room is a mess and I need to wash my hair.' Branquinha moved into the salon towards her room.

'I can help.' Jandaia followed Branquinha.

'I'll change the bed for you,' Pequena offered.

With the room tidy, a bed changed and hair and nails done, Branquinha sat on the porch for the rest of the afternoon waiting for Vilson. It was a Tuesday and not very busy so Dona Branca gave her the night off.

'Pequena, are you sure it was him?' Branquinha asked Pequena.

'Stop asking me. You are beginning to make me think I have seen a ghost,' Pequena answered.

Branquinha missed dinner and only left the porch once for a visit to the toilet. It had gone past eight o'clock when Vilson finally arrived in Jardim do Ouro, washed and shaved.

When Branquinha saw him, he was already climbing the steps of Casa da Branca.

He embraced her and they kissed. People stared at them. Some of the folks assumed it was just lust; others knew.

Zulmira, who had just finished clearing the kitchen and was on her way out, stood next to them. Making the sign of the cross, she whispered to herself, 'May St Antonio and St Valentino bless these two!'

I Will Make Her Happy

The following morning, Vilson didn't go to back to his herd and instead he spent the day with Branquinha. 'I'll wait for them here,' he told Branquinha. 'They will be here before the end of the day and tomorrow morning we cross the river.'

'Don't they need you?' Branquinha asked Vilson.

'My dad agreed to let me hire his foreman. He has been with my family for years and he is driving the cows,' Vilson said. 'With the pick-up truck, things are a lot easier as I can come and go.'

For breakfast, Branquinha made pancakes and they ate at the kitchen table with Pequena sitting with them, reading a comic book Vilson had brought for her and Zulmira, working on the sink, pretending not to hear all the love whispering that was going on.

When they were halfway through breakfast, Carmem walked into the room and, without the usual morning greetings, asked Vilson the question Branquinha had been avoiding all night. 'So, are you taking Branquinha with you then?'

'Carmem!' Branquinha and Zulmira said at the same time.

'He needs to know that you are not on your own!' Carmem looked at Branquinha and then towards Vilson. 'You,' Carmem pointed her manicured finger at Vilson, 'wrote to her saying you were going to live together and her mother could come and live...'

'Go and get your dirty laundry,' Zulmira interrupted Carmem. 'You are coming to the laundry lady with me.'

'Dona Zulmira, if you don't mind, may I answer Carmem's question, please?'

Vilson didn't wait for Zulmira's permission and, looking at Carmem, he replied, 'I'm planning to take Lucinda with me, but at the farm there is only one hut and it has no walls. The men have to wash in the creek.'

He paused for a second. 'I'll come for her when I sort out a room for us, a place where a lady can wash in privacy. We'll also build a stove and an oven.' He placed his hand on Branquinha's hand and pressed it. Turning to Carmem, he added, 'Rest assured, Carmem, I'll do my best to look after Lucinda and make her happy.'

Carmem didn't answer. She moved towards the shelf and picked up the large box of washing powder and the bottle of bleach and left the room.

'Ignore her,' Zulmira said to Vilson. 'She's just protecting Branquinha.'

'Don't worry about it, Dona Zulmira.'

As Zulmira and Carmem left, Pequena lifted her eyes from the comic book and looked at Vilson's face for a while. Then she placed the comic book on the table and said, 'Thank you for the comic book, but I don't want it!' and walked out of the room.

Not a Good Day

Vilson and Branquinha spent the rest of the morning in bed. At lunchtime, she went to the kitchen for something to eat.

'Where's Prince Charming?' Murilo asked without looking at Branquinha.

'He went to get some lunch because after the way Carmem and Pequena treated him this morning I didn't dare to invite him for lunch.'

'Invite him for lunch?' Murilo threw his fork on his plate and turned to face Branquinha. 'Sister, this is not your mother's house that you can invite people to come and have lunch here, you know?'

'Martinho comes and has lunch here and so does Seu Antonio,' Branquinha replied.

'Martinho is Dona Branca's guest. She told him to come and stay here whenever he wants and Seu Antonio is Zulmira's xodó and I'm sure you know the difference between Zulmira and you, don't you?'

Branquinha served herself some rice and beans and poured half a ladle of beef casserole on the side of her plate.

After a while Murilo said, 'You shouldn't be mad at us. We just don't trust this cowboy and we are looking out for you.'

'What has he done for you not to trust him? I don't need anyone to look after me; besides, why was Carmem so rude? And did she need to embarrass me by asking him if he is going to take me away from here?'

'You should be glad she asked because if she had not done so you would still be waiting for him to bring up the subject.'

'I was going to talk to him about it...'

'Were you really?' Murilo challenged Branquinha. 'I bet you were going to wait until he left to find out he wasn't taking you with him.'

'What do you have against him? He has done nothing to you!'

'I don't have anything against him. I'm just wondering when he was going to tell you and what the real reason is he doesn't want you to go with him.'

'For god's sake, Murilo!' Branquinha pushed her plate of unfinished food forward. 'Leave me alone.'

Later in the afternoon, Branquinha came into the kitchen to fetch some water and bumped into Zulmira who was making rice pudding.

'Branquinha, I'm the cook, not your maid. Next time you eat please clear your plate and put it in the bowl for washing up.'

'Sorry, Zulmira.' Branquinha placed the glass under the tap of the terracotta water filter. 'I had an argument with Murilo and I walked out of the kitchen and forgot about the plate.'

'Dona Branca wasn't happy he had breakfast here.' Zulmira poured milk into the pan of rice. 'You must be careful not to upset her because he is not even a paying customer.'

'He paid for the room last time he was here,' Branquinha defended Vilson.

'He did but didn't spend any money on the bar.' Zulmira put sugar into a cup and then into the pan.

'He is not rich or wasteful like the miners.'

'You don't need to defend yourself to me.' Zulmira added more sugar into the pan. 'I'm just worried you might get in trouble with Dona Branca.'

Branquinha didn't reply. She was tired and upset. She poured another glass of water and as she was about to finish, Pequena walked into the room.

'Why were you so rude to Vilson this morning?' Branquinha asked Pequena. 'He was so nice to you. He even brought a comic for you because it is easy to read.'

'What he is doing is trying to buy me and I'm not for sale.' Pequena lifted her chin up and turned her head away from Branquinha.

'What is it with you all?' Branquinha was on the verge of tears.

'Branquinha,' Pequena called just before Branquinha was about to leave the kitchen, 'I know I'm only fifteen and everyone thinks

I know nothing, but I know one thing for sure: if Martinho was allowed to take me out of here, he would not leave me here a minute longer, and I would follow him and live with him under a tree.' Pequena paused for a second. 'If Vilson really loved you, he would have taken you with him today and built the hut walls tomorrow.'

Branquinha didn't answer. She left the kitchen with the glass in her hand, trying to avoid crying.

When Vilson came back, Branquinha told him that she did not mind living in an open hut without a room to herself.

'I could help you build it...,' Branquinha tried to persuade Vilson to take her with him.

'We have waited so long, Lucinda.' Vilson stroked her hair lying on his chest. 'A bit longer won't make much difference.'

Branquinha sighed but she didn't argue that every minute away from him was a minute too long.

Not long before dinner, one of Vilson's men came looking for him. 'I'll go to the camp and see the men but I'll be back later.' Vilson kissed her on the lips. 'I'll have dinner with them,' he added.

When Vilson left, Branquinha had a quick shower and headed to the kitchen. Dona Branca was sitting at the head of the table and clearly not happy, but she didn't say anything.

The silence was heavy, but eventually Dona Branca spoke. 'I hope you are not planning to take another night off tonight.'

'Uhm, I was going to talk to you about this...' Branquinha started.

'Branquinha, I buy your food, give you a roof over your head and look after you, so you are safe from those animals out there.' Dona Branca pointed to the door. 'In exchange, you work here six nights a week. Which part of the deal don't you understand?'

'It would be just today...'

'It is not just today. It was yesterday and if he stays here tomorrow you will want the day off again.'

'Dona Branca...'

'The answer is no.' Dona Branca stood up. 'You work the whole night here or you pay the fine. If you want him to be your last client, fine. But if he is not drinking here tonight, he pays treble for the room!' she said before leaving the kitchen.

Branquinha couldn't eat. She, too, stood up and left the kitchen. 'Don't be upset...' Zulmira followed Branquinha to her room. 'She is worried because we are busy tonight and we don't have enough girls.'

'Zulmira, I feel dirty as it is. How can I sleep with him after laying with four or five other men on the same night?' Branquinha sobbed, burying her head in the pillow. 'It's humiliating.'

'I know, child.' Zulmira stroked Branquinha's hair. 'But sometimes you have to do what you have to do.'

Much later, when Vilson came back and she explained to him that she could not be with him until later he wasn't happy. He cancelled the beer he had ordered and left.

Branquinha spent the rest of the night wondering what was worse, losing her friends, her job or her love. The answer was clear in her mind...

And He Was Sorry

The following day Branquinha woke up to the sounds of the cowboys moving the cows around outside. She got rid of the overnight client and showered as quickly as she could. With her skin not yet dry, she struggled to pull on the blue dress her mum had given her for her twenty-first birthday.

It was a hot day and, as she peeped through the bead curtains of the front door to see if she could spot Vilson outside, she couldn't see anyone or anything other than the cows, moving slowly, heading towards the ferry ramp.

'Very different from last time, isn't it?' Carmem's soft accented voice startled Branquinha.

'Yes.' Branquinha didn't want to lose Carmem's friendship, but she was still sore from Carmem's comments about Vilson.

'It's all about control, you know.' Carmem moved forward peering through the curtains too.

'What do you mean?' Branquinha asked.

'The cows... the cowboys control their lives and they follow them to the abattoir,' Carmem said. 'If we don't take control of our own lives we end up being like them.'

Branquinha didn't reply. She knew Carmem was right.

They stood there for a while watching the cows. Customers from the previous night were gradually leaving, but ended up standing on the porch, as they could not go anywhere.

'The herd is much bigger this time, isn't it?' Pequena joined them. 'Is it all going to Vilson's farm?' she asked Branquinha.

'Only a third. The rest are for the company that bought the abandoned mines up the road,' Branquinha answered.

Pequena moved closer and hooked her arm around Branquinha's. They squeezed past people and leaned against the banister on the porch watching the cows moving and mooing with the occasional shout from one of the cowboys.

'Look, Branquinha!' Pequena whispered. 'It's Vilson at the back of the herd!'

'Oh, my god. What do I do?' Branquinha looked at Carmem.

'You don't have to do anything,' Carmem replied. 'Sit here and wait for what he has to say.'

Branquinha had not told anyone what had happened, but she didn't need to. They guessed.

Later, as the last lot of cows gathered near the river banks, waiting for the ferry to come back, the customers finally left, leaving just the three girls behind.

Branquinha leaned against the banister and occasionally glanced towards where Vilson was, but their eyes had not met.

'*Guapa*, he's dismounting from his horse,' Carmem said. 'And he is heading this way,' she told Branquinha before grabbing Pequena's hand and pulling the younger girl inside.

'Good morning, Lucinda,' Vilson said, squeezing his hat in his hand.

Branquinha didn't move, but she did reply, 'Good morning.'

He cleared his throat before saying, 'I think I owe you an apology for last night.'

'It's all right.' Branquinha wanted to cry.

'Anyway, I acted selfishly and for that I am sorry.'

'Yes, it's all right, Vilson.' Branquinha looked at his face, her eyes staring at his eyes, defiantly. 'I am who I am, and if you can't live with that, you better not come back.'

'You are right, of course,' Vilson replied before asking, 'Can we go somewhere private, please?'

Branquinha and Vilson walked past the salon towards her room. Neither of them noticed Murilo cleaning some mess in the corner of the room.

'And the bastard manages to squeeze in one last shag before he leaves,' Murilo muttered to himself before going back to his work.

No Man is Worth the Sacrifice

Branquinha was waiting for Vilson to arrive any time now. It had been over a month since he left.

'Once the roads are better I'm going to bring a car and some furniture for my house,' he had told Branquinha before he left.

Branquinha had noticed the phrase "my house" but she had not said anything. *They were just words*, she thought, *and after all, it was* "his" house.

The days passed and no Vilson, not even news of him.

'It's a long way and the roads are still bad in some places,' Pequena said.

'It's mid-May, Pequena. The roads are clear and cars are coming from all corners of the country. He should have got back by now.' Branquinha spent most of her days sitting by the porch, waiting for Vilson.

One Saturday night, when the house was full and everyone was busy and fully booked, Pequena knocked on her door.

'Branquinha, hurry up!' Pequena shouted at the door.

Branquinha didn't reply in case her client stopped his business and she would have to start all over again. When the customer left she had her shower and headed for the salon.

'What's got into you, knocking on my door like that?' Branquinha asked Pequena. 'You know what old men are like!'

Pequena looked at Branquinha but didn't say anything.

'I hope you haven't been drinking again!' Branquinha said to Pequena. 'Remember what happened last time.'

'I have only drunk cocktails tonight,' Pequena replied.

'So why were you knocking on my door then?'

'It was...uhm, Vilson,' Pequena said, hesitant.

'Where is he?' Branquinha looked around.

'He's gone now.'

'Gone where? Why didn't you tell him to wait for me?'

'He never came in,' Pequena explained. 'I was outside in the porch and I saw him in a silver pick-up truck. He had a lady in the cabin with him and they looked cozy.'

'What do you mean by "cozy"? Branquinha looked into Pequena's eyes.

'She was sitting very close to him.'

Branquinha ran outside and walked towards the water. It was dark but she could see the shape of the ferry across the river.

'Hello, Branquinha. Tomato and onion on your kebab?' Seu Didi, the streetseller asked, turning the small skewers of meat on the grill over the burning charcoal.

'Thanks but I don't want any kebab tonight.' Branquinha looked at Seu Didi and said, 'Did you see a silver pick-up truck earlier going across?'

'Yes, I did. It was the drover who saved the deaf boy from the stampede,' the old man told Branquinha. 'He crossed about twenty minutes ago with his lady.'

'What do you mean "his lady"?' Branquinha couldn't understand.

'When his worker and the lady got off the car for him to board the ferry, I heard him saying to the man, "Help my wife board the ferry because she suffers from vertigo and doesn't like water".' The old man took a large kebab from the grill and handed it to a customer.

Branquinha didn't understand and she stared at Seu Didi. She started to cry.

'Come on, Branquinha,' Pequena held Branquinha's hand and pulled her gently toward the house. 'Let's go inside.'

When the girls heard the news they, too, were disappointed but not surprised.

'I can't understand. It can't be. Vilson is not married,' Branquinha cried.

'That's men for you,' Carmem said. 'It is time you learn that there are a lot of cheats and liars out there.'

'Vilson is not like that... he didn't need to lie to me.'

'If it's any comfort, he probably lies to his wife, too,' Cloé said and for a change, she didn't sound sarcastic.

'Maybe there is an explanation,' Jandaia said.

'I know there is an explanation,' Branquinha said, more to convince herself than to convince the others. 'I know it.'

'Let's stop talking about this,' Dona Branca said. 'Branquinha, go to your room and have an early night and, next time, remember: no man is worth the sacrifice.'

The Explanation

Branquinha, Jandaia and Carmem were sitting in the salon when Vilson arrived.

'Morning ladies.' Vilson lifted his hat as he greeted the girls. 'I need to speak with you.' He didn't waste time.

Branquinha stood up and looked at Jandaia and Carmem, silently asking them what she should do.

'Maybe you should hear what he has to say,' Jandaia advised her friend.

The explanation didn't come until a couple of hours later when Branquinha and Vilson were lying in bed.

'I know about your wife.' Branquinha finally gathered enough courage to approach the subject.

Vilson pulled her close to him and Branquinha rested her head on his chest. 'It was an accident,' he started.

'What do you mean?' Branquinha lifted her head from his chest and looked into his eyes.

'I had a bit much to drink and I ended up in bed with her.' He laughed a fake laugh.

Branquinha didn't ask any more questions. She knew the deal.

'I see. She is from a good family and I imagine you had to marry her.'

'Yes,' he replied.

'Is she pregnant?' Branquinha needed to ask.

'Oh no, god no! I would not have brought her up to this place if she was with child.'

Branquinha stood up and wrapped herself in a towel. 'Of course!'

'I'm sorry.' Vilson stood up and tried to hug Branquinha. 'I hated doing it and hurting you like this. I'm sorry.'

'I think you had better leave.' Branquinha tightened the towel around her body, holding it close to not fall open.

'Please, Lucinda.' Vilson stood up and put his trousers on. 'How many times do I have to tell you it was an accident?'

Branquinha left the room and headed to the shower.

The Shame

Branquinha sat on the porch on her own, watching the rainwater flooding the street, running down towards the river, and the lightning crossing the dark sky.

Vilson had left for his wife three days earlier and she had since been swallowing the bitter taste of longing for someone she knew would never be hers.

'You will catch a cold out here, Branquinha.' Pequena stood at the door. 'Come inside. Zulmira will make you a hot chocolate.'

'I'm not cold.'

Pequena knelt by the side of the chair and hugged Branquinha. 'One day you will find a good man who loves you as much as Martinho loves me and you'll have his babies and be happy.'

'Don't be stupid, Pequena.' Cloé walked into the porch and sat on the banister. 'She's a whore. Good men never take women like us to be their wives.'

'Branquinha's not a whore, really. She's here only until she gets enough money to start her chicken farm.'

'You don't know what you are talking about, Pequena.' Cloé blew the cigarette smoke out of her lips in one long gust. 'We're all here for the same reason. We all have our own dreams of our own chicken farms.'

'I don't want a chicken farm!' Pequena stood up and crossed her arms. 'All I want is to get old enough so Martinho and I can get married. We might have a few chickens though.'

'You stupid child!' Cloé laughed and walked back into the salon.

'Come on Pequena, go back inside. Your hot chocolate is getting cold.' Murilo appeared at the door. 'Branquinha, you need to cheer up. Depressed girls are bad for business and Dona Branca will not put up with this for much longer.'

'I'm not depressed, Murilo,' Branquinha answered too quickly for it to be true.

'You know he's not coming back. And if he does it'll be just for a shag. The sooner you accept that, the better it is for you.'

'I said, I'm not depressed!'

'I don't care what you say, Branquinha. You need to get your act together and move on.' Murilo pulled the thin, grey wool blanket off Branquinha's knees and started folding it. 'Come and get yourself ready for tonight.' Murilo put the folded blanket in her hands.

Branquinha tried for days to be the cheerful person everyone wanted her to be, but she couldn't pretend every minute of her life.

'Give it a few days; it gets better,' Zulmira said.

'And then what, Zulmira?'

'Life is like this, Branquinha. Sometimes you meet people who you want to keep in your life but then, when they don't want to stay, you must let them go, for your own sake.'

'I know...'

'You should concentrate on making enough money and go home.' Zulmira's black hands squeezed Branquinha's small fingers. 'Not everyone can survive this way of life, my girl.'

Branquinha listened to Zulmira's advice and for the next few days she worked harder than ever. In the afternoons, when girls of easy life were supposed to be resting, Branquinha went to the streets looking for the miners who had not lost all their money the night before and could still afford her services.

'A few more months and I'll have enough to go home,' she wrote to her mother, hoping that it was true. *'With you feeling so much better now and the new pump to help you get water from the well things will be so much easier. I will bring enough money for the chicken farm and with the land fenced and all the other improvements you have already made, we can expand our kitchen garden and start raising hens.'*

As she sealed the envelope, Branquinha closed her eyes and wished the end would come soon because she wasn't sure how much longer she could live with the shame she carried inside herself.

It's All Cabo Ivan's Fault

Branquinha, Murilo and Pequena were cleaning the salon when they saw Sergeant Armando arriving. He struggled out of his car, his belly barely squeezing past the wheel and his face redder than usual.

'Good morning, Sergeant Armando!' Murilo greeted the man.

'Where's... where's Cloé?' Sergeant Armando asked, breathless, holding his heavy body on his arms while leaning on a table.

'Are you all right?' Branquinha asked Sergeant Armando, offering him a chair.

'I need to see Cloé,' Sergeant Armando managed to catch his breath long enough to speak.

'She's still with a client,' Murilo replied.

'Murilo, this can't wait!' Sergeant Armando, still breathless, started walking towards the corridor heading to Cloé's bedroom.

'You must wait, Sergeant!' Murilo stood in front of the large man.

'Get Dona Branca quickly,' Branquinha whispered to Pequena.

'We need to get Cloé out of Jardim do Ouro now.' Sergeant Armando pushed past Murilo. 'Cabo Ivan is on his way to arrest her.'

Murilo didn't need further prompting. He ran towards Cloé's room and banged on her door, 'Cloé, get out. Cabo Ivan is on his way to arrest you.'

'Get out of my way,' they heard Cloé saying to someone inside the room and less than a minute later she came out dressed and carrying a holdall bag.

Get Murilo to take you somewhere to the mines.' Sergeant Armando's face was sweating. 'Pulinho, the ferryman, has a very soft spot for you and if you cross on the ferry now, ask him to hold the

176

ferry on the other side for a while,' Sergeant Armando said to Cloé. 'That should give you enough time to get down to João Preto's mines and hide in there.'

"I am ready now.' Murilo grabbed his keys from the key holder in the bar.

As they started walking towards the salon they saw Cabo Ivan parking the car outside the front door.

'Cloé, go to the back and jump from Dona Branca's bedroom window.' Murilo walked to the front of the salon with Sergeant Armando.

'We've just missed her!' Sergeant Armando shouted at Cabo Ivan, but his eyes were watching Murilo leave the building and climb on the motorbike outside.

'What are you doing here?' Cabo Ivan came into the room and asked Sergeant Armando. 'You said you had to see Capitão Jeremias in Moraes de Almeida.'

'The little bitch took so much money from me over the years that I wanted to have the pleasure to arrest her myself,' Sergeant Armando replied, wiping his red, fat face with a dirty handkerchief. 'And what took you lot so long to get here?' he asked Cabo Ivan and the two other policemen.

'What is going on here?' Dona Branca arrived still in her dressing gown.

'They came to arrest Cloé but when they got here it was too late,' Branquinha told Dona Branca.

'What do you want to arrest her for?' Dona Branca questioned Sergeant Armando.

'Cloé's been a fugitive of justice for a few years,' Sergeant Armando said. 'She killed her husband after accusing him of molesting their two daughters.'

'How do you know all this?' Cabo Ivan asked Sergeant Armando. 'The arrest order only said that she had killed a man by stabbing him fifty times.'

'How do I know "all this", Cabo Ivan?' Sergeant Armando stood taller in front of the thin man. 'I know this for the same reason I was here before you. And that same reason is what makes me a "sergeant".' Sergeant Armando tapped on his chest. 'And you,' he pointed at Cabo Ivan, 'a mere private.'

'Sorry, sir,' Cabo Ivan apologized, his head lowered and his eyes staring at the floor.

Sergeant Armando moved towards the front door, looked outside and turned to Cabo Ivan. 'Now, look what you have done! You held me up and we've just missed the ferry!'

The Invitation

Gringo was lying in Branquinha's bed with his arms behind his neck, one hand holding his own wrist while the other held a cigarette. Now that Cloé had gone away he came to the house frequently and stayed the night. 'Come to Manaus with me for a few days,' he invited her.

'I can't.'

'Why not?'

'Can you see that chart in the wall?' Branquinha pointed to a piece of paper on the wall with two vertical bars drawn on it.

'Yes.' Gringo took a long puff on his cigarette while looking at the graph.

'The blue bar is how much I need to get before I go home and the yellow is the gold I have saved so far,' Branquinha explained.

'How long have you been here?' Gringo asked, pressing his cigarette end on the ashtray.

'Eleven months and twenty days.' Branquinha sighed.

'How about I give you enough to cover an entire month,' Gringo said, getting up from the bed, 'which, according to this graph, would take you to here.' Gringo made an imaginary line crossing almost the top of the graph.

'I can't ask you to give me that much,' Branquinha said.

'You aren't asking, I'm offering,' he said.

When Branquinha didn't reply Gringo went on, 'We'll go to Manaus for a few days and have a break.'

'Why do you need a break? Why don't you go back home for good, instead?'

'I need a break from this place.' Gringo got back to bed, pulling

Branquinha with him. 'And...', he smiled, lying on top of her, 'it's your birthday soon. We could celebrate it in style!'

Branquinha looked at Gringo's smile. 'You are crazy...' She laughed.

Later, they were all sitting around the table having lunch and Zulmira said, 'I've always wanted to go to Manaus. I heard it's very hot, but a beautiful place with many historical buildings.' Zulmira helped herself to some rice.

'Once upon a time, Manaus was the centre of the world because of the rubber in the Amazon,' Murilo told them. 'It was also the only centre for gold in...'

'And he's paying you all that money?' Carmem was not interested in what Murilo had to say about Manaus.

Branquinha nodded, smiling.

'You are one lucky girl, having a holiday and getting paid like this,' Zulmira said, getting up and taking the almost empty pan of rice with her.

'God help you that Cloé will never hear about this or she'll be back here in a flash!' Murilo said. 'I can almost see her face when she hears it.'

'And did you know he even bought new clothes for Branquinha?' Pequena asked Zulmira.

'I did.' Zulmira looked at Branquinha and raised her eyebrows, nodding and smiling. 'With the promise to buy more when they get to Manaus,' Zulmira added.

'I'm missing you already,' Jandaia said.

'It's not that soon, Jandaia.' Branquinha stood up and carried the dirty plates to the sink. 'I can't go until Dona Branca comes back with more girls. June and July are our busiest months and with Cloé gone, I can't go just yet.

'At that rate we will soon have a wedding,' Jandaia teased Branquinha.

'Tell me, Branquinha, will there be a lot of mwah, mwah?' Pequena sat on the table resting her head on her hand and looked at Branquinha, waiting for an answer.

Dona Branca came back a few days later. 'I would have brought three girls instead of two if I'd known you were going away for an entire month,' she said to Branquinha.

'It is not a whole month, Dona Branca. Just two weeks.'

'I thought you said he is paying for an entire month?' Dona Branca looked at Branquinha over her glasses.

'He is paying for the equivalent of a month, but we're only going for two weeks, twenty days max,' Branquinha replied.

'You deserve a break, child. I'm sure we'll survive.' Dona Branca grabbed her handbag and headed to the door. 'The only thing I ask is if you're not coming back, please let me know,' she said before she left.

Branquinha could not hide her excitement. *I'm going to Manaus with my boss. She is going to buy new bedding for the hotel and asked me to come with her,* Branquinha lied in her letter to her mother. *I'll send you a postcard and buy you something beautiful while I'm there. It is a long way from here so we'll be away for about two weeks.*

She packed two new tops and the dress that Gringo had bought for her. 'He said he'll take me shopping in a proper shop,' Branquinha told Carmem.

'What are you going to wear on the trip?' Carmem asked.

'My new jeans and this blouse.' Branquinha showed her a light blue blouse with frills around the collar and at the hem. 'And the new sandals he bought me.' She placed the tawny leather sandals on the bed.

'*Guapa*, borrow my suitcase,' Carmem offered, leaving the room and coming back with a brown leather case. 'I bought it in Paraguay last time I went home. It is new and chic.'

Murilo put his head in the door. 'Woo, almost all ready?'

'Nearly,' Branquinha replied. 'Just finishing here and a shower and I'll be ready.'

'You'd better hurry,' Murilo tapped his watch. 'He's going to be here in less than an hour.'

Branquinha placed a towel on her shoulders before unwrapping the red towel from her head. She finished brushing her hair and put the brush into the toiletry bag, squeezing it into the suitcase and closing the zipper.

Pequena lifted Branquinha's hand looking at her manicured fingers. 'Jandaia did a good job. You look lovely, Branquinha.'

'Like a lady,' Carmem added.

They walked to the salon and Branquinha placed the suitcase by the door with Pequena clinging to her arm.

A truck stopped by the door and for a second Branquinha thought Gringo had changed his car. She only realised what was happening when Carmem put her hand on her mouth and stared at Branquinha.

Vilson got out of the truck and walked up the steps to the porch. They all looked at Branquinha.

'I take it you didn't bring your wife with you,' Carmem said to Vilson.

'I need to talk to you.' Vilson took his hat, off ignoring Carmem.

'Uhm...' Branquinha couldn't finish the sentence.

'She can't speak to you today.' Pequena stood up and put herself between Branquinha and Vilson.

For a few seconds nobody said anything and the silence was broken by Gringo's accented voice coming from the door. 'All ready then?'

Branquinha looked at Gringo and Vilson.

'We'd better hurry, Branquinha, or we will be late for the plane in Moraes de Almeida.' Gringo walked towards Branquinha and lifted the suitcase.

Branquinha didn't reply. She looked at Vilson.

'We need to talk now,' Vilson insisted. 'I made a huge mistake.'

'Didn't you hear what Carmem said?' Murilo's voice was firmer than usual. 'Branquinha, get in Gringo's car.'

'You can't go.' Vilson ignored Murilo. 'I need to speak to you. I want to take you home with me.'

'And what are you planning to do with your wife?' Murilo put himself between Branquinha and Vilson. 'You and Branquinha have nothing to say to one another.'

'My wife is not there any more,' Vilson said quietly. 'Please Lucinda, forgive me. I love you...'

Branquinha turned to Gringo, 'I can't come with you. I'm sorry.'

Gringo didn't answer. He stood there for a few seconds, then turned around and left.

'You can't do that!' Murilo said.

'He loves me,' Branquinha replied.

Branquinha and Vilson were in bed when the truth finally came out.

'Why did she leave?' Branquinha asked him.

'Can we not talk about her, please?' Vilson spoke, pulling her closer to him.

'Are you separating, then?'

'Lucinda, I have asked you, please. Let's not talk about it.'

'No, Vilson!' Branquinha moved away. 'I want to know. I deserve to know.'

Vilson sighed. 'She got pregnant and unbearably unreasonable. She demanded we moved down to the south and sold the farm.'

Branquinha didn't say anything because there was nothing to be said.

'She is capricious and self-centred,' Vilson continued. 'She is using the baby to force me to go back home. I have just arrived here, we can make a lot of money...'

'So she went home on her own then?'

'Yes, can you believe it?' Vilson asked Branquinha. 'When I refused to take her to town, she walked to the main road and got a lift back to Moraes de Almeida and called her father. And when she got there her excuse was that she was not going to put a child in the world to die of malaria.'

'I see...' Branquinha said, seeing a different Vilson.

'Now I have all my family against me and my father is refusing to help, all because of that bitch,' Vilson said, his face pink with anger.

'Do you see what I mean when I told you I made a huge mistake?'

'And what do you want to happen exactly?' Branquinha wanted to know how low he could sink.

'I have to go down south and sort out this mess with her, but as soon as I come back, I will take you to live at the farm with me.'

'And what about your marriage and your child?' Branquinha asked.

'I will have to pretend I agree with her and go there a few times per year.' He turned around leaning on his side. 'But I will spend most of the time with you looking at incredible sunsets every day of our lives.'

Branquinha looked at the man lying in her bed and she wondered if she had ever met a lower creature. 'I don't think this will work for me, Vilson.'

'What do you mean? I thought you loved me!' He stood up and put his jeans on. 'Don't be like that! After all we shared, we deserve a chance.'

'The only "we" I can think of when I think about you is *"We are done!"* Please lock the room when you leave and give the key to Zulmira in the kitchen.'

'Where are you going?' Vilson asked. 'Why are you being so horrible?'

'I always shower after being with a client.' She picked up her clothes from the chair and wrapped herself in a towel. 'Next time you pop into town and want to have sex with me, please ensure you have enough money for the full asking price.' Branquinha turned around and headed to the shower.

Branquinha washed and washed and this time she didn't cry.

Martinho

Branquinha and Pequena were sitting in the salon when they heard Murilo's bike roaring down the road as he climbed the ramp from the ferry.

'Pequena, guess who I've just seen on the other side of the river, getting off João Preto's truck?' Murilo shouted before dismounting his bike.

'Oh my god, was it Martinho?' Pequena asked, throwing her pen on the table and standing up.

Murilo came in, giggling. 'He's almost looking like a man, growing a moustache and a goatee...'

'I need a shower!' Pequena ran towards her room.

'Don't forget to brush your teeth!' Murilo shouted from the door, his voice echoing through the long corridor. 'For all the mwah, mwah, mwah.' He looked at Branquinha and laughed.

Branquinha thought about herself and Vilson. 'Pequena loves him so much, doesn't she?' Branquinha said to Murilo, picking up the pen and pencils and putting them into the small pencil case, her heart crushed inside her chest.

'She does and the best thing is that he loves her more than she loves him.' Murilo nodded his head in approval. 'One day, those two will be happy together.'

It didn't take long for Martinho to arrive. 'Is Pequena in?'

'Good morning to you, too!' Murilo looked at the lanky young man. 'Pequena is in the shower,' he added while wiping down a table.

'Sit here with me while you wait for her.' Branquinha pointed to a chair for Martinho.

'No sitting here unless you are a paying customer!' Murilo said to Martinho pushing the chair back towards the table. 'I didn't finish cleaning this place in the morning and I'm running late. You can help me put the rest of the chairs down.'

'Is Cloé still there?' Murilo leaned towards Martinho and whispered.

Holding one of the chairs up in the air, Martinho looked around the room before he nodded, his eyes wider. 'Cloé said if I told anyone where she is, she'll kill me too.'

'You better keep your mouth shut then, hmm?' Murilo laughed. 'You know who she's in cahoots with, don't you?'

'The last thing I want is trouble with that Cloé woman,' Martinho replied, putting another chair down. 'Especially now I've got the papers to marry Pequena.' Martinho smiled, one of his front teeth missing.

'What do you mean, the papers to marry Pequena?' Murilo stopped wiping the table and came closer to Martinho. 'You're not even eighteen yet and she's only fifteen; nobody will marry you!' Murilo laughed.

'I've got papers.'

'Where did you get papers?' Murilo put his hands on his hips.

'Padilia, one of the miners, had a daughter who died when she was seven and, if she was alive, she would've been eighteen now. He said Pequena could have his daughter's birth certificate,' Martinho explained.

'Your plan is not going to work, Martinho,' Branquinha said. 'When you report someone's death, a letter is sent to the register office where the birth was registered and they update the entry.'

'That's right, Branquinha, but when Padilia's daughter died, they lived too far from the town and didn't have enough money to go to town and register the death.'

'Yeah, that covers for Pequena, but what about papers for you?' Murilo asked.

'I'm eighteen in a month,' Martinho said with a smug look on his face.

'Surely you didn't do all this on your own,' Murilo interrogated the younger man. 'Who helped you to come up with this plan?'

'Uhm… ahm… no one really.' Martinho's voice sounded shaky.

'We don't want Pequena in trouble and this all sounds dodgy to me, Martinho.' Murilo finished cleaning the last table.

'João Preto said we'll be all right.' Martinho straightened his body, looking even taller, 'I want to take Pequena out of this place before she gets pregnant by another man.'

'So when are you planning to marry Pequena then?' Branquinha asked Martinho.

'As soon as possible. I've even got the rings,' Martinho said, pulling two wide, gold wedding bands out of his pocket.

Pequena and Martinho

Branquinha stared at the envelope for a while. She was tired of lies and she wanted to tell her mum the truth. She tore the letter open...

Glória de Dourados, 28th June

> *My dearest daughter,*
> *I was so sorry to hear about Dona Branca's fall and how she could not travel to Manaus. Has she recovered fully now?*
> *I imagine you were disappointed, too. You sounded so excited about your trip. Never mind, my dear, when God closes one door he opens many more.*

Branquinha paused and looked outside. Lies...

> *On the other hand I am ever so pleased you are all looking forward to Soraia and Martinho's wedding and I wish I was there to help you get ready to go the wedding. Talking about weddings, the Pastor's oldest daughter came back from the boarding school and she is getting married. The whole church has been invited and I wish you were here for us to go together. Please send the happy couple my best wishes for a wonderful life ahead of them with many children.*
> *Please, daughter, don't stay there much longer. I'm well and we have more money than we ever had before.*
> *Meanwhile keep safe, sweetheart, and remember, I miss you so much.*
> *With all my love,*
> *Mum*

Branquinha folded the letter and put it back in the envelope. She was glad that not all the things in her letters to her mum were untruths and she was happy for the pastor's daughter.

Three weeks before Pequena's wedding, Dona Branca arrived from Moraes de Almeida and threw herself on a chair, exhausted. 'This is not some massive wedding with five hundred guests, for goodness' sake.' She sipped the water Zulmira put in front of her. 'Can you believe people are objecting to Pequena marrying in a church because she's a prostitute?'

'Do they need to marry in a church?' Zulmira wiped her wet hands on the white kitchen towel.

'Martinho says he wants to marry Pequena in the eyes of the law and the eyes of God.' Dona Branca placed her hands together and looked up. 'Pray for me, Our Lady Mary.'

'What has Father Domingos said?'

'He is away, but I'll go back next week to speak to him. I'm sure he will put sense into those mad people at the church.'

The rest of the week was spent organising the dress and the veil.

'I want it in pale pink with a long veil,' Pequena told the others.

'A long veil is expensive and you barely have enough money for the dress,' Murilo pointed out.

'Dona Branca is paying for the dress,' Pequena said, happy, as if nothing could upset her. 'The seamstress in Moraes de Almeida will have it ready for next week.'

'Still, a long veil is unnecessary and expensive.'

'Murilo, I'll only get married once and I don't want to spend the rest of my life regretting not having a long veil!' Pequena replied with her hands on her waist and a newly acquired assertiveness.

'You have a lot of other things to buy, like...' Murilo paused for a second thinking what were the really important things Pequena needed to buy, '...a sexy nightdress for the wedding night, some nice underwear.'

'Carmem gave me a beautiful black nightdress that she never wears,' Pequena said, excited.

'What about shoes?' Jandaia asked.

'I have my shoes from my first communion,' Pequena said. 'I brought them with me when I ran away from home. I'll show you.' She ran to her room, coming back with a pair of white flat shoes more appropriate for a girl than a bride.

'They are very white.' Jandaia didn't know what to say. 'And pretty...'

'And you have lots of bits for your dowry.' Branquinha came to the rescue. 'All those afternoons spent with the crochet work paid off.'

'With all the gifts we'll get, by the time we get married we'll have a full house.' Pequena could not contain her excitement and kept moving on the floor, twirling around in happiness. 'Did you know João Preto is buying me a cooker?'

'Really?' Branquinha asked.

'He asked me which colour I liked best and I wanted a red one, but Zulmira said I should choose white because it'll show how clean I am in my kitchen.'

The following week, while Dona Branca and Pequena went to see Father Domingos, Murilo and Branquinha visited the large shop in Moraes de Almeida. It sold everything from dresses to mattresses.

'I don't want to buy her a pressure cooker.' Murilo was in a bad mood. 'That's what everyone gets, and she will end up with four or five.'

'Get her an iron then,' Branquinha suggested.

'Branquinha! What does she need an iron for? She is going to live in a hut in the middle of the jungle. Where is she going to plug it in, anyway?'

They wandered around the shop looking for a suitable wedding gift for Pequena.

'How about that jug with the matching glasses?' Branquinha pointed to a tall glass jug up on one of the higher shelves behind the counter.

'Oh, that I like,' Murilo said, watching the shop assistant taking it down from the shelf and placing the glasses, one by one, on the counter.

When they got back to the house everyone compared gifts.

Carmem had got a bale of towels; Jandaia bought a tablecloth and Branquinha a set of sheets and pillow cases. Everyone was impressed with Gigi's generous gift: a pressure cooker.

'I had bought it when I set up house with Davi, but never used it,' Gigi told them. 'It is my contribution to her chance of making this marriage a successful one.'

Pequena had no relatives in Jardim do Ouro, but her friends were not going to let her down.

Two days before the wedding, Sergeant Armando turned up in the house with Cabo Ivan.

'He is here on official business. Get Dona Branca,' Murilo told Branquinha even before Sergeant Armando got through the door.

'We're here to see Dona Soraia,' Sergeant Armando said to Murilo. 'Is she in?'

'Go and get Pequena,' Murilo asked someone and, turning to Sergeant Armando, he said smiling, 'Would you, gentlemen, like a whisky?'

'Yes please, Murilo. Make it a large one for Cabo Ivan here.' Sergeant Armando tapped on Cabo Ivan's shoulder.

'How can we help?' Dona Branca arrived in the room with Pequena.

'We have heard that Dona Soraia, or Pequena, as we know her, is getting married.' Sergeant Armando knocked his whisky back at once. 'And Cabo Ivan here,' the policeman tapped his colleague on the shoulder, 'thinks that, given the age of Pequena, the paperwork must be illegal, so we should stop the wedding and return her to her parents immediately.'

Murilo looked at Dona Branca wondering if she was going to ask him to go into the safe to pay the men a bribe.

'I know Pequena's story, so my immediate reaction was to say no,' Sergeant Armando continued, 'but I have decided to let Cabo Ivan make up his mind for himself.'

Dona Branca pulled Pequena close to her and held the girl's hand.

'Pequena, forgive me my intrusion but would you allow me to lift your blouse and take a look at your back, please?'

'Please, Sergeant Armando, let me marry Martinho,' Pequena

said, crying and turning around.

'You'll be all right, child.' Dona Branca pulled Pequena's top up to the girl's small shoulders, the white bra strap criss-crossing across horrific scars.

Murilo covered his eyes and bent his head.

Branquinha and Jandaia gasped in shock. They had heard about the scars but neither of them had seen them. The lumpy dark skin looked as it was embroidered on to Pequena's thin back, starting from her shoulders and stretching down her back before disappearing down the waist of her shorts.

Cabo Ivan looked at Pequena's back and swallowed dry.

'Show him the iron mark, Pequena?' Sergeant Armando asked the young girl.

Pequena undid her shorts button and lowered it just enough so they could see the "v" shape of the burn mark of a hot iron which had been pressed against her upper hip.

'Did your father touch you like a father should not touch a daughter?' Sergeant Armand asked Pequena.

'Yes.' Pequena's voice trembled.

Sergeant Armando took a deep breath in. 'Cabo Ivan, you are not only a representative of the law in this village, but also an agent of justice.'

Nobody had ever heard Sergeant Armando speaking so slowly and calmly as on that occasion. 'I ask you, do you think it is justice if we send this young woman to the monster who calls himself a father so he can continue to harm her?'

No one corrected Sergeant Armando to point out that Pequena's father had died a few months previously. In fact, nobody said anything. Their eyes were all on Cabo Ivan's face, waiting for his answer.

Cabo Ivan stood up and shook Pequena's hand. 'I hope you have a long and happy marriage, Dona Soraia.' He put his green cap on and left.

On the day of the wedding, the church was full. Pequena had no blood relatives present, but her real family – Dona Branca, Zulmira, Murilo and the girls – were all sitting on the front seats, proud of the bride. Seu Mineiro, Dijé, Seu Leonardo, Seu Geraldo and his daughters were all looking smart in their new clothes.

The father of the groom had finally been persuaded by João Preto that Pequena's past didn't taint her. 'Quite the opposite,' João Preto had said to the man. 'This young lady has been through all sorts of trials and tribulations yet she remained a good and strong person. She'll make a good wife to your son and you should be proud of having such a good woman in your family.'

The party was held in Dijé's Restaurant and when Pequena cut the three-tiered cake covered in white icing and dusted with a thick layer of finely grated coconut and with a large pale pink ribbon around the middle layer, Branquinha's thoughts went back to Pequena's sufferings and she cried. Her tears rolled down her face and as she dried it, she comforted herself in knowing Martinho was a good man and he would look after Pequena.

The following day when Branquinha got up and went to the kitchen to help Zulmira with breakfast everyone was talking about the wedding.

'She looked beautiful,' Zulmira said. 'Everything so romantic.'

'Yeah, so romantic that Seu Mineiro ended up in Carmem's arms.'

'I noticed them dancing.' Branquinha smiled. 'She was teaching him some steps.'

Murilo looked at Branquinha and giggled. 'I can tell you, sister, that last night she taught him a lot more than a few steps. And I'm not talking about dancing!'

'Really? I didn't see anything going on, other than laughter and dancing.' Zulmira pulled the bread out of the oven. 'You watch out what you talk about people, Murilo.'

'You know I can hear everything that goes on in Carmem's room as the walls are this close to mine. They were at it all night.'

'Murilo!' Zulmira rarely raised her voice, but when she did, people knew she was annoyed. 'I don't want to hear any more.'

'We should be happy for Carmem,' Branquinha said. 'Seu Mineiro is a gentle and kind man, just what Carmem deserves.'

The Unthinkable Happens to Branquinha

'Murilo, Murilo.' The entire place could hear Zulmira, the cook, screaming as she hammered with both her hands on Murilo's door. 'Wake up. Branquinha was beaten up and raped!'

Murilo's door slapped wide open and out came Murilo, wearing his football shorts inside out. As he ran up the long corridor with its wooden floor echoing his steps, doors opened and sleepy faces peeped through.

The bedroom door was fully open and Branquinha's motionless body was lying across the bed on her stomach with her face buried in the sheets. Murilo turned her over and put his head on her chest. He could hear her heart, faint, but still beating.

'Get Seu Geraldo, get Dona Branca.' The girls knew that Murilo would never get Dona Branca out of bed when João Preto was visiting unless it was an emergency.

'Is she dead?' one of the girls asked Murilo.

'She's not dead.' Murilo lifted Branquinha's motionless body up and put a pillow under her head. 'Get Seu Geraldo!'

Murilo pulled the chenille bedspread up to her neck and moved a strand of hair from her face, gently tucking it behind her ear. The other girls stood there, some of them sobbing, some just watching, still in shock.

'What's happened?' Dona Branca burst into the room wearing her new black satin dressing gown with a large, green dragon embroidered across the back with its head appearing over the shoulder and the red and orange flames coming towards her chest as if protecting Dona Branca. 'Oh my god, they didn't! Get Seu Geraldo here straight away.'

'We've just found her...' Zulmira was crying.

'Who did this?' Dona Branca demanded, as if anyone knew. 'Son of a bitch. May misery take over his life and disgrace come to him. You will burn in hell, son of Satan!'

'Here is some sweet water.' Carmem came in with a half glass of sugary water.

Zulmira sat on the bed with her wide hips dangerously hanging over the side. She tried to feed the drink into Branquinha's lips, but there was no response.

'I brought some ethanol.' Jandaia gave the white cotton handkerchief soaked with alcohol to Zulmira. While Murilo attempted to wake Branquinha by rubbing ethanol under her nose, Zulmira rubbed Branquinha's bruised wrists with some more ethanol.

João Preto joined them and, to restore some order in the house, he told the girls to go back to their rooms.

'Pray for her,' Dona Branca asked the girls.

Murilo moved the oil lamp from the bedside cabinet and sat on it. 'How could they do that to the poor sister?' Murilo wiped her face with a wet cloth while Zulmira tried to feed Branquinha another drop of the sugary water, this time successfully. 'A man should want to make love to her and not rape her like this.'

When Seu Geraldo arrived there was very little the pharmacist could do. 'There is no point in taking her to the hospital in Moraes de Almeida. The doctor's away for the next three weeks. Luckily, the girl has not lost any blood. She needs to rest and the body will do the healing,' he said as he injected a sedative in her pale arm. With Zulmira's help, he cleaned the blood between her legs.

For the whole day the girls prayed. Their begging voices could be heard through the thin wooden walls. They paced in their rooms, with the rosary in their hands, counting the beads as they prayed to Our Lady Mary and to the Lord Jesus Christ, the Saviour, to help Branquinha. Some of them prayed to Saint Maria Madalena and begged her to help Branquinha to recover.

Zulmira didn't cook lunch as the girls were all fasting, and dinner was meatless soup and bread as penitence to show their contrition to Our Lady Aparecida in the hope that she would plead in favour of Branquinha.

When Guilherme turned up unexpectedly, Zulmira refused to cook him something more substantial and he ate the soup without demanding kebabs.

'Has she told you who did it?' Guilherme asked with his mouth full of bread.

'She doesn't know who it was,' João Preto replied. 'If I ever find out who did it, he won't stay alive for long.'

'She went to bed on her own last night. Her last client left just before we closed,' Murilo said.

Father Domingos could not come that day so at six o'clock that evening, Zulmira turned the radio on, to hear the sacred mass, the blessings of Virgin Mary and the Trinity. By the end of the mass, the glass of water that she put in front of the radio was to be blessed and hopefully that would help in Branquinha's recovery.

Pequena heard the news and came to sit by Branquinha's side. 'Is she going to die?' Pequena asked Zulmira, crying.

'We hope not, my dear.' Zulmira hugged the young girl.

The girls took it in turn to feed Branquinha with the soup Dijé had sent every day.

Branquinha was flying over the small farm where she used to live, her arms open and her lips smiling. She could see the well of her house and the guava trees next to the outside toilet. The huge canopy of the mango trees stopped her seeing through to the old swing where Branquinha had spent many long and warm afternoons. As she flew further up, she saw the manioc plants and the papaya trees next to the pig sty. Her head hurt.

She saw her mum scrubbing clothes on the wooden bench by the banks of the brook all by herself. She didn't deserve it; she had been a good mother. Branquinha tried to go down but she couldn't, and when the clouds came, her eyes were watering and she was no longer above her home.

Still lying in bed in a delirious sleep, she could hear someone's voice in the distance. She didn't quite hear what they were saying, but its sound was soothing. She wanted to wake up, but her eyes were so very heavy.

She went back into a stupor and her mind drifted off to the time when she watched the sunset with Vilson. He had his hat on and stood up in the clouds calling for her, the sunlight more beautiful than ever before.

Branquinha sensed the warmth of someone's hand on her skin and the touch of someone's fingers on her hair. She slowly opened her eyes and saw Pequena's anxious face staring at her.

'Rest, my little angel, rest,' Branquinha heard Zulmira's comforting voice. She couldn't see clearly as it was dark but she knew Zulmira and Pequena would look after her. Branquinha felt her eyes becoming heavy and she fell asleep again, this time with a smile on her lips.

Indian Rosa heard about the rape and she brought some wild herbs which she collected near João Preto's mines so Zulmira could make an infusion to give to Branquinha to make her heal faster.

'They only grow near waterfalls, but they are very good to help in the recovery of people who have had bad injuries and haven't been eating much,' Indian Rosa explained to Zulmira and Murilo.

'I will give them to her at once,' Zulmira said, leaving the room.

'Seu Geraldo kept her asleep for most of the time. She is still very weak,' Murilo told Indian Rosa. 'Zulmira has moved into Branquinha's room so she is being looked after in the night.'

'The man who did this deserves to die,' Indian Rosa said.

'Gui...' Murilo and Indian Rosa heard Branquinha's whisper. 'It was Guilherme... Guilherme did it.' Her head fell to one side in exhaustion.

Murilo and Indian Rosa looked at each other and they understood that Branquinha was in more danger than anyone realised.

'Indian Rosa, you must not repeat this to anyone,' Murilo begged the girl.

'He deserves to die.' Indian Rosa was almost shaking. 'I'll go to prison, but I'll kill the monster!' she shouted.

'Quiet, or you will put Branquinha's life at risk. You are not going to do anything!' Murilo said. 'You go back to camp and tell João Preto what we heard. He'll know what to do.'

João Preto's Manager

'Murilo, there is a woman in the salon.' Jandaia whispered to Murilo.

'God, what is wrong with these people? What sort of place do they think we run? Tell her to go to Eugenia's.' Murilo carried on doing his bookkeeping. 'We don't have dykes in Casa da Branca.'

Jandaia looked at the tall white woman wearing jeans, a T-shirt that had seen whiter days, and a pair of cowboy boots, sitting next to Gigi.

'It might be too late,' Jandaia whispered. 'She is sitting with Gigi.'

'What?' Murilo slammed the calculator inside the money book and shut it closed. 'When is Gigi going to learn to behave?'

Murilo opened the hatch just enough to see into the salon 'Oh, it's Rose!' he said opening the window wider. 'She is João Preto's manager.'

The woman, hearing her name, turned around.

'Murilo!' She stood up. 'How are you?'

'I thought you were coming at the end of the month.' Murilo came out from behind the bar and hugged the woman. 'We have not seen you for ages. What brings you here today?'

'One of the machines broke and I came to get the parts and drop by to see Branquinha,' Rose explained to Murilo.

Rose didn't stay long with Branquinha for the poorly girl was tired and fell asleep again, still drugged by the medicines Seu Geraldo was giving her.

'Is Dona Branca's son around? I have a message for him,' Rose asked Murilo when they got back to the salon.

Murilo went pale. 'Have you heard about him...?'

'I have heard nothing, Murilo.' Rose didn't let Murilo finish his sentence. 'Is he still here?'

Guilherme came into the salon wearing only his underwear and sat on a chair, putting his legs on the table.

Gigi, without saying a word, got up and left the room.

'Gui, we've visitors!' Branca told him off before she left the room. 'I'll get your clothes for you.'

'Murilo, bring me a whisky,' Gui shouted. 'Who're you, flower?' Guilherme scratched his loins and, crossing his legs still on the table, put his testicles on show.

'I'm Rose, João Preto's manager,' Rose replied, unfazed by Guilherme's gross behaviour. 'He said you wanted to borrow some gold from him and he asked me to come to get you so he can give you the gold this afternoon. You can get back to Jardim do Ouro with the miners tomorrow when they finish the mining of the pit.'

'I'll go with you anywhere you like, flower,' Guilherme answered, smiling with his head slightly tilted, his smoke stained teeth showing.

'Gui, my son!' Dona Branca came back into the room with a pair of denim shorts. 'Rose's off limits. Please behave.'

Guilherme laughed, drinking the whisky he snapped from Murilo's hand.

'I'll be back in one hour or so. I'll take you with me then,' Rose said before driving away in the battered black truck.

For the rest of the day and night Murilo couldn't think of anything else but what would João Preto say to Guilherme. Would João Preto beat Guilherme up so badly that he would never turn up in Jardim do Ouro again, or would João Preto cut Guilherme's bits off like he had done with one of the villagers who was caught molesting a young girl? Or maybe he would take pity on Dona Branca and not be so harsh with Guilherme.

Murilo hoped that whatever João Preto did, it would work and that Guilherme would leave Branquinha alone.

When Death is Welcome

Murilo was the first to hear the knocks on the door. He jumped out of bed and, putting his shorts on, ran towards the salon leaving Serginho fast asleep in bed.

'We can hear you. No need to break the door down!' Murilo shouted from the inside, while removing the beam locking the door. 'Who is it?' he asked before he unlatched the last lock.

'It's João Preto.' For a second Murilo froze, wondering why the man was there at that hour in the morning.

'Go and check if Branca is with someone,' João Preto told Murilo.

'No need. Dona Branca's alone,' Murilo reassured the tall black man. 'What happened?'

'Guilherme fell into the pit in the night and cracked his head open. One of the miners found his body just after four o'clock this morning when they went to switch the engines on,' João Preto said as a matter of fact. 'Get me a treble whisky,' he asked Murilo. 'Branca will need it.'

Murilo unlocked the bar and reached for the bottle of whisky, his hands shaking.

'We reported the accident to Sergeant Armando. Rose is in Seu Geraldo's pharmacy waiting while they prepare the body,' João Preto told Murilo. 'Go to Guilherme's room and get some clean clothes and take them to Rose. They will need them to dress the body.' João Preto started heading towards Dona Branca's room. 'Matias is with Zé Carpinteiro making the coffin.'

Murilo was about to wake Zulmira up and tell her the news when he heard Dona Branca screaming.

'My Gui! My son! My only son!' Murilo could hear the pain in her cries.

'What happened?' Zulmira came out of Branquinha's room.

'Guilherme's dead,' Murilo explained. 'He fell in a pit and died.'

'Santa Gertrudes de Nivelles, the protector of the dead, pray for his soul.' Zulmira made the sign of the cross.

'Guilherme will need someone a lot more senior than Santa Gertrudes de Nivelles to get God to forgive his sins, I tell you that!' Murilo said to Zulmira.

Some of the girls and their clients, hearing the commotion came out of their bedrooms to find out what happened, but soon went back to bed. There was no love lost for Guilherme in that place.

When the body was ready, Rose came to get Dona Branca. The girls were all gathered in the kitchen while Zulmira helped Dona Branca get changed to go and see her son.

'So what happened exactly?' Murilo asked Rose.

'Guilherme was very happy that João Preto lent him a kilo of gold to start his business and he drunk a lot of cachaça.' Rose poured some strong coffee from the thermos flask on the table into a small cup. 'No one saw what happened but he must have gone for a pee in the middle of the night and fallen into the pit.' She sipped the coffee slowly.

'That animal died too late,' Gigi said.

'Don't you speak ill of the dead,' Carmem replied.

'This morning we found him lying on the bottom of the pit covered in blood,' Rose continued. 'He must have banged his head on the stones on the way down and again on the machine at the bottom.'

Dona Branca wanted to take the body to be buried in Cuiabá where Guilherme's grandfather was buried.

'We should bury him in the local cemetery,' João Preto advised Dona Branca. 'Gui was a good lad, but he had some bad habits when it came to women. We don't want the police in Cuiabá starting asking questions now that he's not here to defend himself,' João Preto said.

'And if he stays in Jardim do Ouro, he'll be near you.' Rose put her arm around Dona Branca.

They buried the body late in the afternoon and Dona Branca shut the house for two days.

When João Preto and Rose left, Murilo took a long sip of whisky straight from the bottle. He sat down on the little stool in the storage room behind the bar wondering what had really happened to Guilherme.

Leave Before July

It was the first day that Branquinha managed to walk unaided from her room to the porch. Most days, Seu Mineiro or one of the other girl's clients would carry her to the porch and back inside. The bruises on Branquinha's legs were still very sore and she was not strong enough to stand up on her own.

Carmem and Jandaia helped her with her showers every day and Murilo often cleaned Branquinha's room.

'Let me help you with this.' Carmem placed the pillow on the chair João Preto had brought specially for Branquinha. 'I'll go to the kitchen and get the root tea Zulmira made for you with the stuff Indian Rosa brought yesterday.'

The summer had brought many new people and that afternoon, Branquinha sat on her chair, looking at the street and watching people go about their daily lives. Her plans to go before the rainy season came were no longer viable. Branquinha thought about what Sandra Rosa Madalena, the gypsy, had told her: "If you don't leave before July, your mother might not see her daughter alive again."

'How right she was!' Branquinha thought. *'I'm lucky to be alive.'*

Branquinha remembered the latest letter she'd sent to her mother and the lies she had to tell her.

'I won't send any money for a while and instead I will bring it all with me when I come home. This way I don't need to pay any more fees at the gold trading shop.'

Branquinha's thoughts were distracted by Dona Branca coming to sit next to her.

'How are you feeling today?' Branca asked Branquinha.

'Still weak but better than yesterday.' Branquinha answered the older woman.

'Hope the bastard who did it and his entire family rot in hell.' Branca cursed.

'Don't say that, Branca.' Branquinha had not told anyone other than Indian Rosa, Murilo and Rose who had hurt her and now that Gui was dead, there was no point in upsetting Dona Branca even more. 'His mother might be a good woman and have no say in her son's wrongdoings.'

'You are a generous spirited young lady.' Branca stood up. 'I'm going to Dijé to get us some ice cream. What flavour do you want?'

Bring Peace to Those Who Leave

Branquinha was sitting on the porch with Carmem and Jandaia eating the ice cream Branca had got them when she saw Gringo coming down the road.

'Please don't look,' Branquinha asked the girls.

He drove past the house and parked opposite Seu Leonardo's kiosk.

'He saw you,' Jandaia said.

'I asked you to not look!'

'He can't tell I'm looking.' Jandaia laughed. 'I'm wearing sunglasses, remember?'

From the corner of her eye, Branquinha saw Gringo getting off his pick-up truck.

'He's coming this way.' Jandaia got up. 'Come on, Carmem, let's go inside.'

Gringo crossed the road and stepped up on to the porch.

'Hello!' Branquinha decided to face the music. 'How was Manaus?'

'Hot.' Gringo leaned against the banisters. 'You're still here, then?'

'Still here...' Branquinha smiled.

'I thought you were marrying the cowboy,' Gringo said.

'He couldn't get married to me as he is already married to someone else and his wife is pregnant.' Sarcasm didn't suit Branquinha.

'Are you all right?' Gringo asked, looking at the bruise on her forehead. 'How did you get that bruise on your head?'

'Banged into something.' Branquinha wasn't lying.

Gringo stared at Branquinha and, getting up, he pulled her hair back, uncovering the large bruise on her right ear. He gently pulled her shirt away from her neck and saw the strangulation marks. 'Fuck! What have they done to you?'

'It was a few weeks ago,' Branquinha explained. 'I'm all right now.'

'The hell you are all right!' Gringo said, half shouting.

'Please don't make a scene,' Branquinha asked him, throwing the rest of her ice cream in the bin by the porch.

'Have you been to the police?' Gringo lowered his voice. 'You can't let the bastard who did this to you get away with it.'

'He won't be harming anyone, ever again,' Branquinha told him. 'He's dead now.'

'And why are you still here?' Gringo's voice rose again. 'Waiting for the next lunatic to come along to complete the job?'

Branquinha couldn't speak; her throat was blocked with a big knot. She was about to cry and she didn't want to in the porch and in front of Gringo.

As she got up from her chair, and limped inside, Gringo followed her. 'You have to go home. No money is worth this, Branquinha.' Gringo's pronunciation of her nickname always made her smile, but not this time. 'You must go home before you get killed.'

'I can't...' Branquinha started.

'You were not born to live in a place like this. You're making the wrong choice!' Gringo insisted.

Branquinha could no longer contain her tears, her emotions or her anger, so she shouted, 'Do you think anyone is born to do this job? As for choice, we don't have a choice. We're all here because we have to be!' Branquinha sobbed. 'Every person in this house has found themselves in a situation with no choice...' Branquinha sobbed even harder. 'Look at Murilo, Carmem, Jandaia, Zulmira and even Branca, every one of us with no choice but to walk up the steps past that door and do this bloody job!' She pointed to the door.

Gringo didn't reply. He picked up the pack of cigarettes from his pocket and lit one.

'I wish I could go home, I really do.' Branquinha's nose and eyes were red and swollen. 'I have not earned anything this past month and if it wasn't for Dona Branca's charity I'd have nowhere to go.'

Gringo stayed silent.

Branquinha was almost hysterical. 'You tell me I'm making the wrong choice. What choice have I got with legs like this?' She lifted her dress and showed him the semi-healed scabs of the cuts Gui had inflicted on her thighs. 'I spent most of the money I saved on medication and I can't go home ill as I am. That would kill my mother.'

Gringo understood and this time he didn't argue with her. 'I'm sorry... I am so sorry.' He tried to hug Branquinha but she pushed him away. Shaking his head, he turned around and left.

Branquinha collapsed on a chair, her arms crossed on the table and her head buried in them, sobbing, looking at the smoke coming from the cigarette Gringo had left in the ashtray.

'Are you all right?' Murilo came back into the room.

Branquinha couldn't reply or control her sobbing.

'*Guapa*, here is some sugar water.' Carmem put a glass in Branquinha's hand. 'Drink it!'

Gringo came back three weeks later. They were all sitting in the salon, sipping lemonade and hiding away from the heat.

'How are you feeling?' he asked Branquinha.

'Much better, thank you.' She got up and hugged him. 'Thank you so much for paying the bills at the pharmacy. I was so surprised when Seu Geraldo said you were going to pay for all the medication I needed. Please forgive me for being so rude the other day when you were here.'

'That's all right. You had good reasons to be upset,' Gringo replied, putting a rucksack on the table. 'There's enough money here for you to go home,' he said. 'You will never need to come back to Jardim do Ouro again.' He opened the bag and put several wads of cash in front of Branquinha.

Murilo and the girls all looked at the money, then to Gringo and then back to the money. Jandaia took her glasses off, her eyes looking horrifically big while she examined the pile of money. Carmem covered her mouth.

'You can't give me all this money.' Branquinha looked at the notes on the table. 'It's for your farm in Scotland.'

'Branquinha, you've lived here for fourteen months and nine

days and it is time for you go home. You need this money much more than I do.'

There were a few seconds of silence, nobody knowing what to say.

'Can you help Branquinha pack her bags, please?' Gringo asked Murilo and, turning to Branquinha, he said, 'I'm going to put petrol in the truck and I'll be here soon to pick you up and drive you to Moraes de Almeida. I got you a place on the first plane tomorrow morning.'

There was no time for proper goodbyes, but while Carmem and Jandaia packed her suitcase, Branquinha crossed the street to thank Seu Geraldo and his children for having looked after her so well. Dijé was at Dora's across the river, but Branquinha left her a note: *Thank you for being such a good friend. I shall never forget you.*

Branquinha waved to Seu Leonard behind the counter in his kiosk and he waved back.

'Please thank Seu Mineiro for all his kindness and the free apples he gave me the past few weeks,' Branquinha said as she hugged Carmem.

When Gringo returned, Murilo loaded her case on to the back of the truck. Gringo helped her into the car. From the window she waved to everyone on the porch and for the last time she read the sign above the door:

'Our Lord, bless those who enter this house,
protect those who abide here
and bring peace to those who leave.'

THE END

208

Acknowledgements

In life, you never succeed without the help of others and I am grateful to the many people who helped me in my journey to get Casa da Branca researched, written and published.

I would like to thank the girls I met in my time in the gold mining areas of the Amazon, who taught me that things are not always what they seem. Forgive me if I didn't tell your stories well.

In addition, I would like to thank Tom Tomaszewski for telling me I could write and, whether he was right or not, it gave me a huge boost of confidence.

Also, I could not have done this without the valuable input of James Essinger, Hilary Johnson and my publisher Tony Scofield, all of whom not only advised me in so many aspects of publishing but also fixed all my spelling and grammar mistakes, helping this book to be readable.

Finally, I would like to thank David Unsworth, for whose help and devotion I will be forever in debt.